THE GENTLE GUNMAN

The Escorts own a small ranch which has never been anything more than a very poor concern. Nevertheless, someone covets this property and offers are made for it by an agent, though old man Escort is stubborn and refuses to deal. Obviously there is a tricky and deep mystery somewhere in the background. Paul Escort, only son, young and vigorous, stands by his father as the clouds gather round and the storm bursts.

THE GENTLE GUNMAN

THE GENTLE GUNMAN

by

Logan Stuart

Dales Large Print Books
Long Preston, North Yorkshire,
BD23 4ND, England.

British Library Cataloguing in Publication Data.

Stuart, Logan
        The gentle gunman.

        A catalogue record of this book is
        available from the British Library

        ISBN   1-84262-402-4 pbk

First published in Great Britain in 1955
by Ward, Lock & Co. Ltd.

Cover illustration © Faba by arrangement with
Norma Editorial S.A.

The moral right of the author has been asserted

Published in Large Print 2006 by arrangement with
Roxy Wilding, care of Watson, Little Ltd.

Dales Large Print is an imprint of Library Magna Books Ltd.

Printed and bound in Great Britain by
T.J. (International) Ltd., Cornwall, PL28 8RW

For

Tom and Marcelle

CHAPTER I

The Escort Ranch

In the shadow of a scattering of gnarled and ancient cottonwoods lay the Escort place: a small horse ranch squatting some half-mile back from the broad trail which ribboned through grama grass and then, winding itself around the boulder-strewn land to the east, flung out finally towards the desert and the border lying south.

Westwards, behind the 'dobe ranch-house, with its broken-down wood outbuildings and corrals, grass stretched for a short distance until meeting up with the boulder rock of the foothills. And, beyond those thinly wooded hills, the Smoke Signal mountains rose in lofty beauty, their white-capped peaks seemingly brushing the sky itself.

Pine, juniper and aspen stubbled the mountain-sides in a patchwork of varying greens. To the north a distant line of willows, cottonwoods and brush bisected the country here from east to west, marking the course of the winding Rio Chico. On the far bank of the river lay the town of Lariat. It was almost as though the frontiersmen and traders who had founded the town had taken one look at the country south and had said to themselves, 'We either build this side of the river or not at all.'

For a fact, except for the one hundred and twenty acres of grassland owned by the Escorts, the county was rough, broken and hostile. And beyond the sweep of the Smoke Signals, sometimes in the hills themselves, the Apaches lived, rode and hunted, and periodically broke out to plunder a house, an outlying ranch, a small wagon train.

The Escorts had been here five years, and only once had a few bucks tried to raid the ranch. That had been as far back as three years, and the over-confident sons of more cautious fathers had met with such accurate fire from a single deer rifle and a solitary six-gun that they had lost three of their small band within the first few minutes. Wisdom, to some extent at least, was learned in those few moments – a wisdom bought of bitter experience – so that the plan of attempting to steal any of the geldings in the meadows and corrals was immediately abandoned.

The remaining eight Apaches, having gathered up their fallen brothers, had fled, not because they were cowards, but because they feared the wrath of their leaders even more than the accurate firing from the house. They had had no business to be away from their camp in order to raid, because at that time there was 'peace' between the whites and Apaches. An uneasy peace, whose very existence was jeopardized by the periodic depredations, singly or concertedly, of either white or redman.

But of long late there had been no sign of Apaches, and the Escort household, with no common enemy to unite them, fell back upon bitter words and sometimes silent brooding. Harsh and unjust things were said by both husband and wife, and sometimes, *sotto voce*, by their daughter Sarah. Only Paul, their first-born, seemed able to hold himself aloof in these arguments and scenes of unhappy recrimination. Certainly he must have felt a hurt within him at these times, for no true son can condone family strife or remain entirely immune from the burn of hot words.

He spoke rarely, for the work of the place, small though the ranch was, fell more and more on Paul's strong shoulders as William Escort slowly, defeatedly, relinquished his hold on the reins...

This spring night the lamps had been lit and, thanks to Paul Escort's labours of the last few days, a good fire burned in the stove against the chill of coming night, and a plentiful supply of wood lay neatly piled by the back door. And, with his day's work done, Paul sat with a much-thumbed and treasured book, straining his eyes to absorb yet again the printed words in the yellow glare of the single oil lamp.

The others still sat at the table, their empty plates pushed to one side. William Escort packed an ancient pipe with dry-as-dust tobacco. Sarah, coming up seventeen, gazed boredly around the kitchen, speculating on what chance she might have of attending the next dance in Lariat.

Martha Escort sat for a moment, pushing her greying hair from her care-worn face, mentally poising herself to tackle the chore of clearing and washing the supper things.

She regarded her husband obliquely, feeling pity and anger at the same time. 'Why,' she said, as she had done so many times past, 'we had to pick a place like this, I don't know. This trail leads to nowhere. How many horses have you sold in the last six months, William? One,' she went on, answering her own question, 'and that for a miserable forty-five dollars!

'Whoever comes this way except men escaping from the law, riding lathered horses and forcing you almost at pistol point to trade a fine black gelding for a wretched, spavined, wind-broke crittur–?'

'Mr Twitchell comes sometimes, Ma,' Sarah said, bringing her thoughts back from the romantic atmosphere of a dance. 'He's nice, I think–'

'Mr Twitchell! Well, I don't think he's so

nice,' Martha Escort said. 'There's something I don't like about him. Still and all, that's no reason why your father should turn down such a right good offer as Mr Twitchell made us for this broken-down place!'

The elder Escort stirred in his chair. He had so many sharp retorts on his tongue he couldn't find the right one to use in reply.

He said, after a pause, 'You know as well as any of us, Martha, why we came here. Five years ago, jest over, mebbe, we met an army man in Mescal, remember? They were going to build a fort down here, south of the river, so he said. Ideal for a horse-breeder, he said, if a man can produce good geldings for army remounts–'

'Why,' Martha asked, 'did we have to take the word of a drunken trooper? That's something *I* should like to know–'

'We all took his word at the time, didn't we?' Escort reminded her angrily. 'Sarah was too young, but it was put to Paul because mostly he would be workin' the ranch. You were ready enough to pack up our things, sell out and quit Mescal for this opportunity! How could any of us foresee the army wasn't fixin' to build their fort here at all?'

'A pity we didn't find out fer sure,' Martha replied bitterly. 'But now we've got the chance to sell out to Mr Twitchell, why don't we take it, William?' Her voice lost something of its bitterness and belligerence;

she managed to infuse a wheedling note into it.

William Escort was again silent for a while. How could he explain to his family that to sell out now would be the one final admission of his own failure? And how or where could he start again with no more than a thousand dollars or so capital and the few horses that were left to them?

He looked across at his wife and was suddenly struck by the haggard face and poverty-haunted expression. Twenty-one years ago Martha had been a young, lovely and vivacious girl. Now, at thirty-nine – or was it forty? – she looked a tired old woman. *Almost,* William Escort thought, *as tired and old as myself!*

'Pa figures its too late to make another start,' Paul said quietly, looking up from his book and surprising his family, as he often did, with this odd perspicacity of his, for penetrating quickly and simply to the heart of a problem.

He went on in his deep, soft voice, 'It would take considerably more than a thousand dollars, Mother, to start up afresh. Time we paid off what we owe in town for grain and such like–'

He had stopped talking suddenly and had moved with such speed and with such liquid grace that before anyone could bat an eyelid he was out of his chair and had plucked the deer rifle from the wall and was holding it ready.

'Someone coming,' he told them quietly, and only then did they hear the soft hoof beats still some way off in the night.

They listened for a moment; a silent, frozen tableau, only their eyes moving and turning to this broad-shouldered young giant who, in such moments, instantly assumed a natural-born leadership.

'One rider only,' Paul said in answer to the question in their eyes. 'But it could be a horse-thief or an outlaw.'

He indicated the single lamp as he strode to the door with a fantastically light step.

'Turn the lamp down, Father, until I get outside…'

Martha half rose from her seat, bitterness now turning quickly to anxious concern. But, remembering how Paul had dealt with the Apache raid three years back, when he was but seventeen, she sank back.

William turned the lamp down so that the flame almost flickered out. When he looked up, Paul had gone outside without sound or obvious movement.

They waited in the semi-darkness and presently heard sounds near to the house. A horse nickered and bridle chains jingled, and voices came low but clear across the night air.

This, then, was no skulking enemy or

thief, else Paul would have shot and called out his warning.

William Escort turned up the wick and shortly the door opened. Paul came in, carrying the deer rifle in his big-boned hand. He brushed the long fair hair back from his forehead, holding the door open for the visitor.

Red Twitchell entered, closed the door softly, almost furtively, behind him and gave the room the benefit of his wide and disarming smile. It was a pleasant face unless one noticed that the smile did not reach the cold, green eyes.

'Why, Mr Twitchell!' Martha exclaimed rising. 'Have you had supper? Yes? Then let me fix you a cup of coffee.'

Red nodded, still smiling. He looked at Martha and William, and then his cold gaze caressed Sarah's face with warm appraisal. Only Sarah noticed it, and flushed with pleasure.

'A good thing for me I ain't a hoss-thief or some such,' Twitchell said. 'That boy of yours musta had me covered from the first cottonwood way across the yard. Like an Injun,' Twitchell finished. If insult or compliment were intended, Paul Escort gave no sign as to which he favoured. He regarded the tall, rangy rider with his gentle, fathomless grey eyes.

'Glad to see you, Twitchell,' William

Escort said belatedly, and waved a hand to the spare rocker. 'Set, while Martha fixes you some coffee.' Escort ran fingers through his iron-grey hair and tugged gently at the spade beard, regarding the tall, handsome visitor speculatively.

'You come to make me another offer, mebbe, Twitchell?' he asked as Red took the proffered cup from Martha.

He stretched his long, booted feet and crossed them and smiled again. He was, as always, quietly but expensively-dressed for a range rider. His black stetson, which he had now removed to reveal his red thatch, though trail-dusty, was of the best. Likewise corduroy jacket, woollen shirt, whipcord trousers and hand-tooled spurred boots. Around his neck was a black silk bandana with a white polka dot. Around his lean hips, visible beneath the unbuttoned jacket, was a filled shell-belt; the butt of a Colt's six-gun protruded from the oiled-leather holster.

'As a matter o' fact,' Red said slowly sipping his coffee and reaching for his makings, 'I have.' He rolled and lit the cornhusk paper *cigarrito* and blew smoke contentedly, aware that he had the studied attention of everyone, even Paul. *Perhaps,* he told himself, *this is the right moment at last.*

'Like I told you folks before,' Red Twitchell

said, addressing himself mainly to the elder Escorts, 'I'm nothin' more than an agent fer a business syndicate. Cattle, hosses–' He waved a hand airily. A hand which, for all its owner's fine clothes and air, was sun-blackened and rope-calloused. Paul Escort had noticed this before.

'For business reasons the syndicate don't want to advertise itself. You *sabe?*' He smiled at the father, and William nodded, although he could not understand the need for mystery in such a business as this.

'What was it we offered you before, Escort?' Twitchell asked as though such details were the last things that he and the syndicate concerned themselves about.

'A thousand dollars for the place as it stands an' title deed of the land,' Escort said. 'That wouldn't include the geldings, naturally.'

'Naturally,' Twitchell agreed smoothly. 'The syndicate's got its own stud horses for breeding as well as English white faces an' long-horned Scottish cattle.

'But they see possibilities in this strip, Escort. Things could be done by a syndicate with considerable resources. Irrigation and such like.' Again he was suitably vague on details.

'Things that a man like yourself, runnin' a one-man, or' – he glanced at Paul – 'two-man outfit, couldn't start to do.'

Martha said, her glance bright on Red's face, 'What's this latest offer, in terms of cash, Mr Twitchell?'

Paul had replaced the deer rifle in its rack on the wall. Now he carefully watched the face of this man who dressed well and rode a fine horse; this man who had work-roughened hands like a rider, *yet who did not ride for either Hackamore or any of the smaller outfits north!*

Twitchell rose now, stubbing out his cigarette, his gaze ranging from one face to another, settling a little longer on Sarah's flushed cheeks before reaching Martha.

Although he was careful to make his offer to the head of the house, his cold green eyes continued to watch the changing expressions on the lined face of Martha.

'The syndicate's given me the power to offer you two thousand, Escort, for the ranch as it stands and, of course, a transfer of the land title. We don't figger to include your stock or personal property in that, of course.' Red gave a half-rueful smile, disarming enough for his audience to see, or imagine they saw, simple honesty of purpose.

He laughed shortly, now playing his trump card.

'Of course, pushing the figure up to double the previous offer means I lose a good bit on the deal myself. Oh, sure, I get my normal percentage,' he assured them, 'but could I have bought for less the syndicate said for me to take the balance – up to a couple of thousand.' He shrugged, still smiling, maintaining the attitude of a good loser in a fair business deal.

'As I see it, the place is worth that much – not to you folks, but to a big organization that can afford to spend and improve. That's why they's willing to go so high.' He turned to Escort now, reaching for his hat and clamping it on the back of his red thatch.

'You don't haveta decide right now. Guess mebbe you'd like to figure a few angles – where you'd go, how much capital you'd have if you was to sell the horses. Reckon we might find you buyers for them geldings so you could raise the ante to three thousand, mebbe.

'I'll be ridin' by in the morning, and I don't have to tell you how smart you'll be to settle–'

'Why,' Martha cried, 'we wouldn't get another offer like this in a hun'ed years–'

Red nodded, 'You've hit it, ma'am. Reckon mebbe your family'll see it that way too by tomorrow.'

He pulled at the door latch and turned, wishing them good-night as he flashed them his ready smile. Sarah's glance dropped as she read the *personal* interest which Red seemed to bestow on her. William nodded and Martha gave a high-pitched nervous laugh. *This was more than she had dared hope for; surely William would agree?*

Only Paul's face remained empty of expression as he crossed the room as silently as a cat and followed in the footsteps of the mysterious Red Twitchell...

The room was alive with chatter when Paul returned nearly a half-hour later, but there was something in his face which caused Escort to halt the babble of talk with a commanding motion of his hand.

Martha looked up from her chair, and William said quietly. 'What is it son? Something to do with Mr Twitchell?'

Paul sat down and spread his hands in front of him, looking at them, big and strong and work-worn. Then his glance lifted as he regarded his parents thoughtfully.

They were still unaware, he considered, in spite of the heavy work he did, that he was now a grown man. This talk which he had interrupted – they had not waited for him to come back, but had begun their discussions, their see-saw arguments over Twitchell's offer. Maybe already they had decided to accept. In Martha's eyes he read the suggestion of victory, yet glancing now at the stubborn lines in his father's seamed face and the near defiance in his eyes, Paul wondered whether his mother's triumph might not be premature.

'Twitchell was not alone,' Paul told them quietly. 'I figured in the beginning that I'd heard another horse in the distance.' He paused and let his calm gaze flicker to the still flushed face of his sister. He saw now, suddenly, many things to which before he had been blind. Not blind, perhaps, but groping and uncertain. It looked like Twitchell was making a play for Sarah, and unconsciously Paul flexed his shoulder and arm muscles so that the shirt tightened on his upper body and gaped at the neck to expose his bronzed, corded throat.

'Ace Charro was along with Red tonight,' he said. 'Keeping in the background like a skulking coyote. If Red keeps company with a man like Charro, this syndicate he talks about could be no more than a bunch of desperadoes and footpads–'

'What are you saying, son?' Martha cried, but William waved her to silence.

'Ace Charro?' William repeated thoughtfully. 'Now where in blazes have I heard that name before?'

'Charro was Hackamore's range boss until a coupla years back,' Martha put in quickly. 'Frank Kearney fired him on account there was some talk of him being in with outlaws or rustlers or some such. Don't reckon they proved anythin' as I mind it, but Frank gave him his time fast enough. There was all kinds o' rumours in town at the time.'

Paul nodded as though he had known all this – which he had – but scarcely considered it worthy of mention.

'If Twitchell's in cahouts or friendly with Ace Charro,' Paul said, 'then it's a likely thing that this syndicate only exists in Red's mind, or at best is a collection of owlhoots, else why all this secrecy? Twitchell hasn't told us a thing about this business.'

'If there was no legitimate syndicate behind the offer,' Escort said slowly, 'how would folk like Twitchell and Ace Charro – if they *are* in cahouts – raise so much *dinero*?' For almost the first time in his life Paul was being consulted on equal terms. His opinion asked for in something of grave importance. He realized this without any feeling either of triumph or bitterness. It was something he accepted quietly, assuming this weight of responsibility with no more than a mild surprise.

'I'm sure Mr Twitchell wouldn't do anythin' wrong,' Sarah said. But the interruption was ignored as it contributed nothing constructive to the question under discussion.

'That roan gelding of his is worth all of three hundred dollars,' Paul said. 'You know that, Father. He sits a good Visalia rig, his clothes are good and so are his guns. Yet,' Paul paused significantly, 'far as we know he doesn't ride for any spread in the whole valley.'

'Meaning?' Escort asked, shaggy brows drawn together.

'Meaning,' his son said quietly, 'that unless he's got a *private* source of income, he must be making money some dishonest way. Even was he working, no forty-a-month hand could lay two thousand dollars on the line and still spend like Twitchell does.'

'How do you know about what he spends, Paul?' Martha said, suddenly subdued.

'Anyone in town will tell you,' Paul replied. 'It's common knowledge–'

'Common knowledge or common gossip?' Sarah demanded hotly.

Paul regarded her seriously and with anxious concern. 'When I go into town,' he told her, 'I talk to folks most times, not only Harvey at the livery, but others. Twitchell spends a good deal of time in the Yucca Saloon. It was said only a week or so back he lost a thousand-dollar pot in a poker game.'

This was a long speech for Escort's son and he now relapsed into a thoughtful silence.

'Did they see you when you followed Twitchell just now?' Escort asked with apparent inconsequence.

Paul looked surprised and smiled, gently shaking his head. 'I didn't want them to,' he said simply.

He stood up then, a towering figure in this low-ceilinged 'dobe house. He said, 'I'll make a round of the stables and corrals and have a look at the geldings.'

When he was gone, Escort turned to his wife. 'I don't reckon we'll take Twitchell up on this, wife. I don't like it!'

Martha sat staring stonily ahead, her face bereft of its former animation. She said nothing...

CHAPTER II

At the Yucca Saloon

Twitchell and Charro, once well away from the Escort ranch, put their horses to a fast run. The young moon was already in the sky and cold bright starlight helped to illumine the trail.

After a time they pulled in their mounts for a blow and rolled *cigarritos*.

Ace Charro, dark faced, dark of eye, turned his gaze to Twitchell as he blew smoke from his thin nostrils. In Charro was a trace of Indian blood. He knew cattle and horses like nobody's business. He was deep, untrustworthy, and, like some horses, had a mean streak right through him.

'You figger they'll sell out at two thousand, Red?' he asked, and added, 'Bigawd! they better had. It's too much, anyway! How we goin' to raise it–?'

Twitchell smiled. 'Charlie'll cough up the main amount. That's *his* problem. We do our share an' more, ridin' the seats off our pants.'

Charro nodded. 'Like you say, Widgeon had better shell out. It's us as does the rough work–'

Twitchell grinned at his companion in the moonlight. 'It won't be long now, Ace, before we can cash in. We got the buyers an' we know where the cattle are. Let's get along to town, *pronto.*'

Such was the horseflesh they had under them that within two hours the lights of Lariat twinkled ahead. They could see the silvery river gleaming between the trees and where the brush thinned out. Around the town itself, across the Rio Chico, most trees had been felled within a half-mile radius and the timber used for building the town.

They racked their dusty mounts in front of the Yucca and batted alkali from their clothes before crossing the boardwalk and pushing open the swing doors.

Inside, they took in the familiar pattern, seeing it through the eddying whirls of tobacco smoke under the bright hanging lamps.

They bellied up to the bar, thirsty and eager. A few men nodded and grinned at the newcomers, and Gib Little, one of the bar-

26

keeps, came forward with bottle and shot glasses. 'Boss said for you to go straight through, Red,' he said.

Twitchell swallowed a drink. 'Jest as soon as we've washed down some o' this goddam dust.'

They both had a second drink and Red planked two silver dollars on the counter, wiped his mouth on his cuff and turned, leading the way to the door at the end of the long bar.

He saw Corinne at the roulette table and winked at her. She looked pretty good, he thought, in that low-cut yellow dress, her pretty shoulders revealed and her black hair cascading down in ringlets.

She smiled, and then her full red lips pouted as Red and Charro moved straight on to the door, opening it and closing it softly behind them. Corinne, annoyed, returned to her job of calling for bets and spinning the wheel...

Inside Charlie Widgeon's private office, Red and Ace Charro helped themselves to chairs, toeing them up to the table where Charlie was already seated, scribbling something on paper. He greeted them and pushed a bottle and glasses towards his henchmen. Finally he rose, put the papers on his desk against the wall and returned to his chair, lighting a cigar and puffing blue-grey smoke with every sign of satisfaction.

He was a big man, inclined to fat. His dark hair was worn slicked down with a cow-lick over his temple. Dark eyes looked out from fat lids and his fleshy face was bisected by long, waxed moustaches.

His glance travelled from one face to the other. He said: 'Well, Red, do we get the Escort place without any – huh – trouble?'

'I ain't certain sure, Charlie, but I figger they aim to close the deal. Hadta to give them till tomorrow to talk it over.'

He paused, and Charlie Widgeon, noting Twitchell's hesitation, asked: 'Anything else, Red?'

The tall, red-haired man drew out his sack and expertly rolled a *cigarrito*. He blew smoke before replying.

'I ain't sure, Charlie; they's somethin' about thet kid I don't cotton on to–'

'What kid?' Widgeon demanded sharply. 'If you mean the boy, let me tell you he ain't no kid. He's sure enough grown up in these last months.'

'Yeah! I reckon mebbe he has, and I ain't never noticed it 'till tonight–'

Widgeon stared. 'It's your job to notice things like that, Red. What is it you don't like? You figure young Paul Escort as a trouble-maker?'

'Could be, Charlie, now you come to put it like that,' Twitchell said slowly. 'I guess I don't like the way he looks at you, like a sick

28

cow, jest a-lookin' an' sayin' damn-all!'

Ace Charro spat disgustedly. He glanced at Red, but spoke his mind to the owner of the Yucca.

'You got any ideas this kid might gum up the works, Charlie, say the word an' I'll run him through one dark night.'

Widgeon did not care for Ace Charro's easy familiarity, but he reminded himself that a man could not always be choosey over his tools. Sometimes he had to use the ones which came to hand and Charro was, after all, a useful man. He held a burning grudge against Hackamore and Frank Kearney in particular. That alone made him worth something. That and the fact that Ace knew every mound and hillock of Hackamore range and also the outfit's method of working!

Red said, reflectively. 'The kid's growed some since I saw him last. I reckon you're right, Charlie, he ain't a boy no longer. We'll watch it.

'Like I said, Ace an' me'll ride out early tomorrow morning and get their final word. Best show 'em a few hundred dollars as a token, I guess–'

'I'd already thought of that,' Widgeon said coldly. 'Leave the figuring to me, Red. I'll give you five hundred to take in double eagles. The sight of that much gold should make 'em decide fast enough. If not' –

29

Charlie Widgeon paused impressively – 'we'll haveta be a little more drastic. How long,' he asked, turning to Charro, 'before Hackamore rounds up its first gather for the spring drive?'

Ace rubbed his saddle-leather face with a lean hand. 'Last coupla spring round-ups, since I quit,' he said, 'they done the same thing at the same time, and I don't know any reason why they shouldn't again, 'ceptin',' he added cautiously, 'Frank Kearney's bride-to-be's already arrived in Lariat, as you know. *That* might alter things a mite, though I don't figger so, really.

'Ain't no reason, far as I can see, why Jed Segal – Kearney's ramrod – shouldn't get on with the round-up same as before. Kearney wouldn't be ridin', anyways.'

Widgeon nodded. 'All right. Suppose they work to the same schedule as before, in spite of Kearney's forthcoming marriage, what then?'

Charro drained his glass and regarded Widgeon through his narrow lids. 'They'll round up at least a thousand critters an' haze them to the holdin' ground, south of the Chico, and to the north-east of the Escort ranch. They won't figger they'll need more'n two-three night-hawks to watch that bunch, there bein' no Injun scare an' precious little rustlin' – at the moment!' He grinned and trickled tobacco smoke down his nostrils from a freshly lit *cigarrito*.

'Reckon Segal will be startin' in almost any time now,' Charro continued. 'That bein' so, they oughta have a good gather inside a coupla weeks. Beef critturs mostly, an' mavericks, they'll've combed out an' be ready to brand.'

Again Widgeon nodded. He took a huge timepiece from his vest pocket and consulted it. It was a gesture to impress these men, though Charlie Widgeon himself was not objectively aware of it, and would have been angrily surprised if anyone had the temerity to question his motives.

'You can put your hand on enough riders when the moment comes, Red?'

'Sure,' Twitchell said, 'easily, but a little honey might keep 'em sweet till we're ready to move. One-two of the boys are getting bored and most are down to their last *peso*.'

Widgeon sighed, withdrew the cigar from his mouth and placed it in an ash-tray. 'How many?' he asked. 'And don't forget they gotta be men who'll take orders from you and Charro without question!'

'We can put our fingers on eight riders who'll do like they're told jest so long as they get their cut. They're as good with guns and knives as they are with cattle.'

Widgeon nodded, thinking, *Border scum who would slit each other's throats for* un peso fuerte!

31

'And the cattle buyers?' Widgeon asked, studying his men through puffed lids.

Charro said, 'They'll pay around ten dollars a haid for prime beef on the hoof an' mebbe five fer mavericks–'

'Accordin' to what Ace said,' Twitchell broke in, 'there should be something like eight hun'ed steers an' a coupla hun'ed mavericks. Eight thousand plus a thousand, Charlie; nine thousand dollars fer one night's work!'

'Not quite so simple an' straightforward as that, Red. I've already spent quite a sum on this thing. They's your cut and Charro's as well, an' each of eight riders is going to receive two hundred once the beef is safely across the border.' He withdrew a pencil from his vest pocket and jotted down figures on a piece of paper.

'It's goin' to cost close on three thousand time the boys and you two are paid up,' Widgeon told them, 'and you'd better make the rounds tonight and give each rider a coupla gold pieces. Tell 'em to stick around and be good and ready when you need 'em. You, Red, and Charro, get an extra cut for keeping my name out of this from the word "go." Agreed?'

They both nodded and sealed the contract with another drink.

Widgeon bent down in front of the combination safe, twirled the knobs and presently returned to the table with two leathern pokes, both of which he handed to Red.

'The heavy one, of course, is for the Escorts. There's three hundred and twen'y dollars in this other one, forty dollars for each of your riders. They get the balance when the job is done.'

Red nodded, but Charro said: 'How about us, Charlie?'

'You'll be coming in tomorrow,' Widgeon replied. 'You can have an advance then. But jest don't let any of those hombres get drunk. We can't afford having some fool shoot off his mouth, *sabe?*'

'Leave that to me, Charlie,' Red said, rising and stuffing the pokes into his shirt. 'We'll have one for the road on the way out an' then hit the hay.'

They came out into the now noisy and jam-packed saloon and had their drink before beginning their last chore of the day: that of scouring the deadfalls of Lariat in search of Red's eight owlhooters...

Paul Escort, watching the square of darkness begin to pale, stirred himself and sat up slowly, brushing straw from his upper body.

This square frame, in which the desert stars were now barely winking, was the unglazed window in the small 'dobe stable adjoining the house.

Close to Paul's head, within easy reach,

the deer rifle lay as it had done every night now ever since the Apache attack. The practice of sleeping in the small stable with the wagon team had begun then, and the habit had grown into a permanent routine.

In the beginning it had been as a precaution against a sudden night attack, because here Paul was able to absorb all the night sounds, both natural and alien. There was little chance of an enemy sneaking up to the house, or a horse-thief approaching the corrals and meadows beyond the house so long as Escort slept in the stable. And although there had been no trouble of that kind since a Mex had tried to steal a gelding and Paul had sent him on his way with a well-aimed shot, nevertheless, young Escort held to his practice, preferring his present sleeping quarters to the stuffy and overcrowded 'bedroom' inside the house – Paul's bedroom having been the kitchen-living-room with the sofa as his bed.

He rose now and brushed the remainder of the clean, sweet-smelling straw from his clothes and went outside, filling a bucket from the pump.

He placed the bucket on the bench, stripping off shirt, and doused himself in the ice-cool water, drying himself on the towel which he kept in the stable.

He replaced his shirt and buckled the leather belt around his flat belly, returning to the barn, where he shaved in front of a cracked and fly-blown mirror. Afterwards he ran a comb through his waving, blond hair.

He filled another bucket from the pump and took this inside the house, depositing it near the stove. Paper, shavings and wood from the box soon had the stove roaring away. He filled a kettle and placed it atop, alongside the family-size coffee pot.

Sounds from the next room told him that the family were beginning to stir. At least, he smiled to himself, not Sarah, probably, who was never too good at dawn rising!

The essential domestic chores completed, Paul returned to the stable, where he forked a little hay into the manger and fed the two shaft horses the last of the grain.

The spring wagon was kept in a nearby ramshackle shed, and, presently, Paul would hitch the team up, grease the axles in preparation for the drive to town. More grain was needed as well as stores for themselves, and he wondered how much *dinero* his father would be able to spare this time.

It did not seem to strike Paul in any way odd that he should shoulder the burden of the ranch work and receive no payment. If the thought of riding for Hackamore or one of the smaller valley spreads had ever entered his head, he had dismissed the idea by reasoning, simply, that his parents and sister had need of him here.

Yet, as he smoked a *cigarrito*, he felt vague stirrings in his breast. Not for the first time did he let his thoughts wander into the realms of the fanciful. He supposed that, at the back of his mind, he had always had a nebulous idea of helping out in some more ambitious way. That was why his little spare time was spent with the few treasured books. Few folk knew, or even bothered to consider, that Paul Escort had taught himself many things. He could speak the border Spanish with the fluency of any *vaquero;* he had an amazing natural aptitude for fast and accurate shooting, and although, with the exception of the three Apaches, he had never killed a man, wild game of all kinds, from a buck to a crow, had fallen to his .22 rifle.

He stood outside, watching the sun come up over the desert, and, as always, he felt strangely moved. There was a beauty here which no words could describe and which no artist could adequately portray. It gave him a feeling of utter tranquillity and peace as he watched the bright colours come and go and soften, finally, as the sun moved slowly upwards into the bluest of skies.

He dragged his gaze away at last and sat down on the bench near the pump, thinking now of what lay ahead.

Although the last word had yet to be said on this question of selling out, Paul felt sure in his heart that his father's mind had been made up last night. And, in a way, Paul could understand and, oddly enough, was glad that his father was being stubborn about this as he had been before. He would not sell, Paul was certain, even for two thousand dollars, because William Escort had neither the initiative nor the physical ability to start life afresh in a new place.

And, as Paul himself had pointed out last night, there was something funny about Red Twitchell and his offer! Paul's glance ranged over the corrals and grassland, where the geldings, thirty of them, were cavorting in the early morning air. *They* were worth something, he thought, if you could find buyers, but who in their right senses would pay two thousand dollars for a 'dobe house and shacks and a hundred acres or so of grass, even if it was grama?

He heard the rattle of dishes and, hungry now, went inside to join the family at breakfast.

'Well,' William Escort said, stirring sugar into his cup, 'it's sure enough decided, I reckon, like it mostly was last night. We ain't movin' out o' here, Martha and Sarah, and that means we tell Twitchell "no" when he comes.'

'But–' Martha began.

'It's not jest on account neither Paul nor me *likes* Twitchell,' Escort interrupted. 'Wish it was as easy as that. But we don't want dealin's with sech men – rustlers, mebbe, or even outlaws–'

'Nothin' like that's been proved or even suspected,' Martha pointed out reasonably.

'True, we have no proof of that, neither would we spread such gossip abroad; it could be plumb dangerous. But you heard Paul tell you this Twitchell don't work, yet he's got money to lose at poker an' kin own a hoss worth three hun'ed dollars at least, beside a hun'ed-dollar saddle–'

Escort wiped his mouth and beard with a red handkerchief. 'There's other reasons, too; like we wouldn't *have* two thousand time we settled our credit in town. There wouldn't be enough to start over again, I tell you, Martha. We cain't even sell the geldings without hazin' them fifty-sixty miles to Fort Union, then we got no guarantee the remount officer would buy!'

'Perhaps yore right after all, William. I guess I was stupid ever to hope we could quit this desert country.'

There was little more to say after that, for, though the decision had already been taken, Martha herself was now in agreement, seemingly. Paul had had his say and young Sarah would, albeit, abide by the word laid down by her parents.

What this rejection of Twitchell's offer was going to cost, in flesh and blood, no one of the Escort family could possibly foresee...

CHAPTER III

Corinne

Paul whipped the team up into a steady trot along the wide, ragged trail northwards. It was only seven o'clock, and the heat was not enough to worry the horses yet.

Around Paul's waist was strapped his father's cartridge belt and Colt's gun. Always Paul felt a little self-conscious when carrying a gun in town. Out here in the wild, broken country it was different. It was not unknown to meet a Mex or a white man who needed a fresh horse or money or both and was prepared to throw down on you. Besides, more than once Paul had a shot a rabbit, sometimes even a quail or a roadrunner. That was something in itself to do such a thing with a six-gun at extreme range; added to that was the fact that something extra for the pot had been produced out of thin air and for no more than the cost of a single or maybe a couple of bullets.

Paul tapped the pocket of his shirt, assuring himself that the list of requirements was still in his pocket. A battered sombrero shaded his head from the sun's mounting heat, and with little need to guide the trail-wise team Escort slumped easily on the wagon seat, relaxed and yet, like an animal, unconsciously alert and watchful.

Though his eyes were almost closed, he still would not have missed the slightest movement in the mesquite clumps; nor would his ears fail to pick up the slightest sound which might presage danger or untoward movement.

But nothing disturbed either the tranquillity of the land or of Paul Escort. He had half expected to meet Red Twitchell on his way out to the ranch, but here was Lariat a hundred yards beyond the road-bridge and no sign of the man. If he had ridden out already, then he must have taken a more circuitous route, and that would be across the dog-leg section of Hackamore's most southerly land; the vast basin wherein many of their steers were held before the spring and fall trail-drives...

The wagon clattered over the road-bridge, travelling slowly now as the first shacks and buildings came into view. It was the middle of the forenoon and Lariat was having a busy time.

The town was laid out in the usual pattern, except that it could boast three inter-sections crossing Main. Otherwise the business and trading section lay at this southern end, and saloons, honkey-tonks and the like lay sandwiched between these and the small residential section beyond.

Paul drew up at Al Harvey's livery and feed barn and, sure that there was no obstruction, tooled the wagon inside through the high, wide doorway.

Harvey, a thin, serious-faced man in a sweat-stained shirt and waist overalls, nodded amiably.

He wasn't too happy about the Escort's bill, but he rather liked this quiet, unassuming son.

Paul wound the reins round the brake lever and sprang from the box in a single, cat-like bound. He grinned back at the hostler, pushing back the battered hat and looking at Harvey with a mixture of guile and innocence.

Harvey regarded his customer balefully, yet knowing all the time he would let the boy have *some* grain, even if he didn't settle up for the order before last.

'How's our credit, Al?' Escort said. 'Don't tell me, I know. Low as a sidewinder's belly.' He laughed then and fished into his pocket, producing the handful of golden eagles which Escort senior had given him out of the fast-dwindling store.

Al Harvey blinked. 'Reckon that about puts you in the clear, Paul.' He took the money and then, as an afterthought, stuffed one twenty-dollar piece into Escort's shirt pocket.

'Don't go cleanin' yoreself out, son,' Harvey said, lighting a thin cigar and carefully extinguishing the match. 'Come back in an hour an' I'll have the grain sacked for you.'

Paul regarded him for a moment and then, with a softly muttered 'Gracias, amigo,' turned and came out on to the street, threading a way through riders and vehicles towards the hardware store which lay next to the Yucca saloon, from which it was separated merely by an alley.

Escort paused with one foot on the boardwalk as Corinne came through the Yucca's bat-wing doors. He paused for three reasons. Firstly, it was unusual to see Charlie Widgeon's entertainer abroad at this time of day; secondly, Paul had a secret admiration for her deep down inside him; thirdly, a drunk had appeared from the same swing doors and was holding Corinne's arms with unnecessary strength and bending his head down towards her lips.

Paul did not know the big, bearded man, nor would he have bothered had he been Governor of the Territory – a most unlikely thing. But what Escort could see of the byplay he did not like.

Obviously the man had been drinking, yet he was steady on his feet and in no way reeled as most drunks did. It so happened that there were few folk at this particular spot. A small knot of idlers gossiped nearby but seemed unaware of anyone excepting themselves.

Escort hesitated and looked at the girl. Without her revealing yellow dress in which Paul had seen her but once, and now gowned almost conventionally in a day dress of the period, she looked even more lovely than Escort remembered.

But these thoughts and emotions flashed through him with the speed of lightning as he saw that the man was not only hurting her, but trying to kiss her publicly.

She wrenched her head round in an effort to escape the stubbled mouth, and Paul saw her white face turned towards him. In her eyes there was an appeal, but she would not call out and fought down the desire to shout or scream.

She was powerless in the man's grasp, yet she hesitated to involve an outsider in her trouble.

This, Escort sensed in his strange, intuitive way, all within a matter of seconds, and like a piece of darting quicksilver he moved, but with far more force and effectiveness than a globule of mercury.

In a moment he was on the board-walk and easily, almost gently, had broken the man's hold by the simple and effective procedure of gripping both biceps and exerting the full, steely strength of his big fingers and hands.

The beard-stubbled one let out a squawk of anguish. Flames of pain shot through his arms. He was as helpless as a hog-tied steer for branding

Corinne stepped back and watched with a breathless, wide-eyed wonder as Paul lifted the man bodily and hurled him on to the street almost under the feet of a rider's horse.

The rider swore and neck-reined his mount with commendable dexterity. He started sounding off, and then stopped abruptly as he realized that the youngster on the board-walk must have pitched the fellow bodily.

The rider, one of Bart Reed's BR6 men, grinned. 'Next time you start in throwin' *hombres*, pitch 'em *over* me and not *under*.' He glanced down at the big man, who was slowly climbing to his feet, and gigged his horse on down the street.

Paul's breathing was perfectly even, his face calm. He smiled as the BR6 rider went by and quickly transferred his gaze to the man he had thrown.

Jack Cotter had never before met up with a man who could do such a thing to him, least of all a kid! It was this almost shocking realization which caused a slowing of his reflexes, so that when he went for his gun he was perhaps not quite so fast as usual. Still and all, he was faster than most.

Corinne let go her breath in a rush, her

word of warning coming hard on the heels of the sound of scuffling boots. In a second or less the idlers had scattered and the three principal characters stood against the background of sun-drenched buildings and slowly eddying dust.

Cotter's gun was already clear of leather before Paul moved. The onlookers blinked once, and during that short space of time they saw the pale spurt of flame and heard the crash of a six-gun. But only one gun! And the flame and exploded bullet had issued from the Colt held in the big, steady hand of the Escort kid!

'Hell! He ain't a kid any longer,' one man breathed. 'He's a full-growed man an' more!'

Cotter's gun lay in the dust, where it had been sent by Paul's fast and accurately placed slug. He stared stupidly at it as he flexed the number fingers on his right hand.

Escort's gun was sheathed, and no one had seen him replace it in the worn and sagging scabbard.

It was Corinne who voiced the doubts of the onlookers.

'He'll shoot again, kid–'

Paul's calm smile choked off her words as effectively as a gag. 'The cylinder's damaged so it cain't revolve, Miss Corinne,' he smiled. 'He won't harm us, I'm sure!'

Cotter bent to retrieve his gun. One glance told him that what the kid had said was true. The gun would not fire in its present condition. There was the thinnest sliver of fear in his eyes as he gazed malevolently at the kid who had thrown him with such amazing ease. Then, with a low-muttered curse, Cotter returned the damaged gun to its holster and turned sharply on his heel, making his way to the end horse at the hitching rack.

Corinne, marvelling still at what she had witnessed, began to feel the shakes of a reaction.

'I guess I need a drink, kid,' she said. 'Come in and have one yourself – on the house.'

Escort hesitated. He drank but rarely. The last time, he supposed, must have been when he had purchased a bottle of rye for his father two-three weeks back.

The girl caught his arm in a gentle grip. She could feel the muscles ripple in his forearm, and suddenly Escort grinned down at her and said, 'I'm not much of a drinking man, Miss Corinne, but I guess it would be plumb discourteous for anyone to refuse such an invitation.'

Again she looked at him with something of wonder in her wide eyes. Corinne, in her profession, had met many men and many types. All men could be pigeon-holed and labelled according to the category into which they fell.

She was not at all sure, however, that this Escort could be dealt with so simply.

They passed inside, and Corinne, her hand still on Paul's arm, shepherded him over to the long bar. The men ranged along the counter had only just returned to their drinks, having with one accord moved to the doors at the sound of that single shot.

They had seen Cotter retrieve his damaged gun and the picture was clear to their astonished eyes.

Now they mostly nodded and grinned in friendly fashion as Paul stood by the bar. They eyed him with deep respect. Like one man outside had said, this boy of William Escort's was no longer a kid, and quickly they set about revising their ideas. He was offered several drinks, most of which he refused. One or two whiskies, especially at this time of day, were more than sufficient for Paul Escort.

It was Corinne who told them in terse sentences what had transpired, and in spite of her strictly accurate version, Paul felt strangely uncomfortable at the admiring glances and compliments bestowed on him.

'Any man as kin throw Jack Cotter has got my respect,' Gib Little drawled as he refilled Corinne's and Escort's glasses. He leaned forward slightly over the counter and spoke

47

directly to the young, blond giant. 'Better watch out fer that Cotter hombre, Escort,' he warned. 'Wouldn't put it past him to snuck up on you one day – or night – 'specially when he's got a few drinks under his belt.'

Paul nodded his thanks. 'I'll remember that.'

Corinne turned her head, looking up into Paul's face. 'So you're Paul Escort. I couldn't place you at first, although I figured I'd seen you in the town once or twice.'

Escort smiled. 'That's right, though I don't come in so often excepting just for supplies. Our ranch is nearly thirty miles south of the Chico, you know.'

'I remember now,' Corinne said, 'you breed geldings, and you have a young sister; is that right?'

'Sure,' Paul said. 'What's more, we just had an offer from a hombre called Twitchell – Red Twitchell; know him?'

She nodded, surprise making her face appear softer, less sophisticated looking.

'I should know him,' she returned quietly. 'I – we – but what was in this offer? You don't mean he–?'

Paul said in his simple direct way. 'He said he was an agent for a big syndicate dealing in cattle an' horses, and although they didn't seem overmuch interested in buying our geldings, Twitchell figured to pay us two thousand for the land and the 'dobe house an' outbuildings.'

Corrine's breath came out slowly.

'Two thousand dollars?'

'You don't seem to figure it's worth that amount of *dinero*,' Paul grinned. 'Cain't say I blame you, either, considerin' we payed a dollar and a quarter per acre.'

'Are you sure, Paul?'

'Sure on both accounts, Miss Corinne,' Escort replied soberly. 'I know what my father paid and I know what Twitchell has offered us. Fact is, he's probably along at the ranch now, getting our decision.'

'And are you – your father–?'

He said, 'It's too late for my father to start some place else.' He paused, thoughtfully, wondering why he was telling all this. The ugly thought came, unbidden, that Corinne might well be Charlie Widgeon's woman, and if so it did not seem quite right for him to be talking and drinking with Corinne in Widgeon's own place. Paul couldn't figure out why, he just *felt* it.

He pushed the empty glass away, refusing another drink.

'I've got stores to buy. If you'll excuse me, Miss Corinne, I'll be on my way.'

She walked with him to the doors, aware that the eyes of the men at the bar were more on young Escort than on herself.

'You're – you're going to stay there,' she said. 'You've decided not to sell to Twitchell.'

49

It was a statement, but Paul, looking at her, nodded and smiled.

He said, 'Isn't it this Saturday that Frank Kearney's getting spliced? Maybe if I come to town I'll see you again?'

She looked at him, slowly shaking her head, her eyes moist. She yet contrived to return his pleasant smile. 'Don't you go befriending a saloon girl, kid. I'm not your kind, though I'm deeply grateful for what you did a while back.

'You see, there are few men, if any, who would have tackled Cotter like you did. Yes! Kearney's getting married on Saturday; his bride-to-be is staying over at Trail House.'

'Well,' Paul said, 'I guess the whole town'll turn out on Saturday. My sister wants to see the wedding. Maybe I'll bring her along–'

'Then you certainly won't talk to me,' Corinne flashed. 'Leave well alone–'

He was constantly surprising her, and now, again, he did not fail. He took her hand and gave a slight, courtly bow. His white teeth gleamed against the contrast of sun-blackened face, his fair hair fell forward over his brow, and his eyes, as usual, were calm and steady.

'I don't think that because you work in a saloon you are damned to Hell's eternal fires,' he said gravely.

She could not be sure whether he was serious or mocking. Then she looked again and felt sure that, in spite of his light tone, the sentiments expressed were profoundly sincere.

She moved out with him on to the walk and touched his arm lightly as her gaze travelled across and down street to where Trail House stood.

'There *is* Rona Jefford,' she told him. 'Frank Kearney's betrothed – just crossing the street.'

Escort's glance followed in the direction Corinne indicated.

Even at that distance, and in bright sunlight, he was able to observe her exquisite beauty. His sudden stiffness communicated itself to Corinne, and she swung her gaze back to his face, watching him with mingled feelings.

She turned abruptly, retracing her steps into the saloon, yet Escort remained staring across the street, scarcely aware that his companion had gone.

He saw that Rona Jefford's hair, visible below the tiny velvet bonnet, was the exact colour and texture of corn-silk. Her dress appeared to be of some dark grey material, yet cut so exquisitely that it enhanced every facet of its owner's natural beauty.

She held the trailing skirts as she crossed the dusty street before ascending the board-walk on this side. After that she became lost to view in the throng of people on the walk.

Paul Escort, standing there, wondered when he had ever seen a thing of such rare beauty, and suddenly felt guilty at such thoughts. In Escort's eyes, Rona Jefford was already as good as Frank Kearney's wife, and for that reason he had no right in gazing so *longingly*–

He was about to move, conscious of having wasted more time than he should, when a voice hailed him from the middle of the street. He smiled as Marshal Rich Toomis came forward and stepped on to the walk alongside him.

'Well, kid,' the marshal said in a dry voice, 'looks like when you *do* come to town you sure give the pot a stir!'

Paul studied the seamed face of Lariat's lawman, speculating for a moment on the meaning of his words. Then he smiled. 'You mean that little ruckus with the unshaven hombre? What did they say his name was, Jack Cotter?'

'Yep, to both questions, son,' the ex-Indian Fighter replied, his rather mournful gaze flitting over Escort's well-muscled body. 'Seems like I ain't the only one who had better quit thinkin' of you as Escort's kid.

'I didn't see what happened, but I sure heard about it. If I wasn't so sure you could take care of yourself I'd say watch out, Escort, fer Cotter and his breed.'

Paul smiled at the diplomatically worded

warning. 'I don't want to appear rude, Marshal, but I guess I'd better get my supplies and hit the trail–'

'Wait a minute,' Toomis grunted. 'I got me an idea, if you can spare a moment an' step into the office.'

Paul regarded the marshal quizzically and shrugged. Why not see what Toomis had to say? And as for getting back to the ranch quickly – well, he wouldn't make it now in time for dinner, anyway.

Inside the office, Toomis sank into a chair at the desk and indicated a vacant one for Escort.

'It jest occurred to me, Escort,' Toomis said, hunching arms and shoulders over the littered desk, 'that mebbe you could do something fer me and at the same time earn yourself a few *pesos!*'

Escort was puzzled, but he waited for the lawman to explain further.

'There's gettin' to be a sight too many range-lobos drifting into town lately,' Toomis explained, 'and Lariat's council figger to appoint a night marshal to take over from me every night.' He grinned. 'Even an old Injun fighter has to have some sleep now and again.'

Paul nodded. 'You having much trouble here, then?'

'I can smell it comin',' Toomis said. 'Hombres like Cotter an' Ace Charro to name a couple. They're no-good drifters, but they don't drift on! But mostly I'm worried about Saturday and Frank Kearney's weddin'. Town's goin' to be plumb full, an' Kearney, like most big ranchers, has got plenty enemies–'

'Like Charro, for instance?'

'Yep! And others I could mention. Wouldn't take much to start somethin' with half the Hackamore outfit along–'

'Are you suggesting,' Paul said, 'that an old Indian campaigner like you cain't handle a few drunks?'

'I'm suggestin' I may not be able to handle Trouble on my lonesome. It ain't allus jest a question of a few drunks. They's shootin' at times like this, sometimes in fun, an' then all of a sudden a hombre gits serious about it an' folks git hurt, usually innocent bystanders.

'Further, I'm suggestin' that for the day you might help me out an' git paid mebbe five-ten dollars for yore trouble. I ain't *seen* you in action, but from what I heard I reckon you could'a killed Cotter two-three times over afore you shot at his gun. *That* sort of fast action, son, is most likely to keep Lariat on its feet durin' Saturday's festivities.'

'Well,' Paul said, surprised and embarrassed at the offer, 'I guess I could use ten dollars, and I was fixin' to bring Sarah along for the dance in the evening.

'She wants to see the wedding, anyway, so

it would only mean coming into town an hour or two earlier, wouldn't it?'

Toomis nodded his grey head. 'I was hopin' you'd see it that way, Escort. Reckon I kin persuade the councillors to cough up a ten spot extra for the day, and I sure cain't be in every place at once.'

'Well,' Paul grinned, rising to his feet, 'I'm no gunfighter, but I'll sure keep my ears and eyes open an' mebbe earn that money.'

'It's Kearney you gotta watch closely, an' anyone as might take a pot shot at him. With a big crowd here, the conditions is favourable to sneakin' coyotes, even though half of Kearney's outfit most likely'll be trailin' along!'

CHAPTER IV

A Near Thing for Kearney

The team had been rested and grained at Harvey's livery and were eager enough to take the trail for home at a smart pace.

On the wide and less rutted stretches Paul let them out, but where brush and boulders narrowed the trail and made for more difficult going, Escort let them walk.

He had eaten at one of Lariat's Chink

restaurants, and now the wagon bed was pretty well stacked with bulging grain sacks and stores and groceries for the family.

He had been forced to pay cash for one or two items – shells for the Colt's deer rifle – but generally had been allowed more than the usual credit.

The story of how young Escort had, with consummate easc, bested and actually thrown the redoubtable Jack Cotter, had enhanced him in the eyes of most of Lariat's store-keepers. Thus Paul had found that so long as he had been willing to answer their questions and satisfy their starved natures by recounting the story, however simply, they were more than ready to consider this a sort of payment in kind.

In fact, it was mostly the townsfolk themselves who had retold the story to Paul himself, merely waiting now and again for his nod or head shake to help them along with the recital.

The very fact that this youngster from below the Chico was so deprecating and absurdly modest about the episode lifted him, in Lariat's eyes, higher still from the usual run of tough hombres. The funny thing about this Escort kid was that he didn't *look* so tough. Not when you studied his calm eyes and face. Only when you noticed the rippling muscles, visible at his neck and underneath his shirt, his long sloping shoulders and the feline grace with which he walked and moved, only then, perhaps, did a man begin to realize that this quiet, almost gentle, kid possessed unplumbed depths.

Lariat was used to listening to braggarts like Jack Cotter, Ace Charro and, to a lesser degree, Red Twitchell. To hear them talk sometimes you'd think they were Sam Houston, Jim Bowie and Davy Crockett all rolled into one. But then *those* men weren't talkers; they were the doers of this world. And already, unknown to young Escort, and through that simple episode with Cotter, Paul's name had been compared with that of the already fabulous William Bonney, better known as Billy the Kid. But those who had made the comparison had done so with intent to compliment and not insult. For Bonney, already a gunfighter of repute and still only a boy, spent most of his time, in between stealing and killings, in eluding Sheriffs' posses.

Escort would have laughed had he heard the talk going on behind his back, understanding with his direct simplicity that the most truthful westerner was prone to exaggerate, and loved to build a legend around any likely candidate.

He was nearly to the half-way mark on the trail indicated by the single giant cottonwood on his right and the distant scattering of *saguaro* trees on his left, beyond the dog-leg section of Hackamore. That was when he saw the rider ahead and instinctively knew, even before recognition made it certain, that the man was Red Twitchell.

They approached slowly, and when they met each man pulled in and stopped.

Twitchell's gaze flickered to the piled-up stores in the wagon bed and then returned to Escort's face. His mouth quirked in a smile, but there was no humour in his eyes.

'I'd figgered *you*, at least, Escort, had a grain of sense in your head, but I guess you ain't no smarter than yore Pa!'

'Meaning, I suppose,' Escort said softly, 'that we're all crazy not to sell out to your *syndicate?*'

There was a subtle emphasis on the last word and Twitchell glanced sharply at Escort's face. Red felt a sudden surge of anger and fought it down. *This is not the moment to pick a quarrel,* he thought; *soon the young fool will be sorry they didn't sell. Then it'll be too late!*

Now Red shrugged and matched Paul's calm with a forced coolness of his own.

'Reckon it don't matter a lot,' he said. 'I kin see by your load you're sure fixin' to hang on here. Ain't yore folks ever scairt, livin' down there on the desert edge away from other folks?'

Paul said softly, 'If we can handle Apaches I guess we can handle anyone else who figures to steal horses or make trouble.'

Again Twitchell gave the boy a sharp glance. He wondered whether there was any underlying significance in Escort's words. He made a mental note, there and then, that whenever the deed was done he would see that Paul Escort was well out of the way at the time!

Paul said, wickedly, 'Figured you'd have your saddle pard along with you – Ace Charro.'

He saw Twitchell's sudden start, but almost immediately the man recovered himself. 'No, not today,' Red said, forcing a smile. 'Mebbe I'll see him in town.' He nodded, lifted the reins and spurred his fine gelding forward before Escort could make answer.

Paul turned on the wagon seat and watched until the rider became a distant, dust-enveloped speck.

He smiled to himself and clucked the team into motion, holding them to a steady pace until at last they swung into the Escort yard.

Sarah Escort had but one party dress, and that was a frilly affair made of muslin which Martha had made for her two years back on her fifteenth birthday.

Sarah had unearthed it from the trunk and had studied it critically and with a feeling of bitter disappointment. Even if it were pressed and had new ribbons threaded through the puff sleeves and neck, it would still look dreadfully old and, now, too childish.

But the problem had been solved in an unexpected way, as problems so often are, although, even then, from Sarah's point of view, it was not entirely satisfactory.

It was the fact that Paul had accepted Marshal Toomis's offer – the proposition to be a deputy for the day – which at once made the wearing of a party frock impracticable for young Sarah.

Paul would have to get to town early in the forenoon if he were going to keep a sharp look-out for drunks and possible gun trouble. That meant that Sarah could not possibly parade herself all day in a dress which was only suitable for the dance Lariat was holding in the evening.

True, Sarah might ride out with Paul in range clothes, taking the dress with her and changing into it later at Trail House or at the house of one of her few friends. But her brother had argued that there would be lots of girls and women at the dance clad in their work-a-day clothes, and that a neat buckskin skirt, shirt-waist and Justin boots would be by no means out of place.

Reluctantly, Sarah allowed herself to be persuaded, and certainly her parents would not countenance her making the long trip to town later in the day *without* Paul to accompany her.

It seemed, then, that the best plan was for the both of them to wear range rig and use saddlers. That way they would make the trip easily in two hours instead of the three or more hours it would take by wagon.

Martha said, anxiously: 'Look after her, Paul. I ain't too happy about this job you've gotten yourself. How you figger you're goin' to keep an eye on Sary *and* do a marshal's job?'

'Don't fuss, Martha,' William Escort said as he sloshed whisky into a glass, avoiding his wife's disapproving glance.

William Escort was feeling more relieved in his mind since Twitchell had been given his answer two days ago, and had, presumably, accepted the decision philosophically. Escort felt that a load had been lifted from his shoulders, and as the whisky coursed through him he began to think seriously of how to get buyers for the geldings out there. They were getting fat and lazy, and cropping the fresh grama grass down, particularly in the corrals. He looked at Paul now, awaiting his answer to Martha's question.

'The dance isn't until tonight,' Paul said quietly, 'and by that time Kearney and his bride and riders will be long back to Hackamore. Toomis is only worried that someone might try making trouble while Kearney's in town–'

'It sounds a dangerous job,' Martha said, 'and what'll Sary be doing while you're walkin' the town, lookin' fer trouble an' – mebbe gettin' yourself shot or somethin'?'

Paul said patiently, 'Sarah will be at Trail House, maybe even visit a friend or two. She won't be out on the street except for while Kearney and Rona Jefford are inside the church getting married. Later, when it's time, I shall take Sarah to Al Harvey's big barn where the dance is being held. She'll be amongst friends right until I bring her home!'

Martha's worried gaze shuttled from one to the other of her 'children.' Sary *did* look kinda sweet and pretty, standing there in her long, divided skirt, a spotless white shirt-waist and her golden-brown hair loosely held by a red ribbon.

Sarah said, 'I'll be all right, Ma. So will Paul. Guess mebbe he kin look after himself better than you all figure.' It was surprising that the youngest member of the family should have realized something which the others as yet but dimly sensed.

The parents watched as Paul buckled on his father's gunbelt and examined the loads before slipping the six-gun into its holster.

Sarah spent some moments titivating herself before the mirror, and Martha, with a sudden lump in her throat, saw herself as she had been years ago, before near poverty and the hot, hostile land had dried her blood as effectively as it had slowly consumed her hopes.

And, likewise, the father regarded this calm, poised son of his, sensing some of the latent strength within him, both mental as well as physical. No longer were there any personal ambitions in the breast of William Escort; only for the boy who would, assuredly, perpetuate his father's hopes and succeed where the older man had failed.

These were indeed gloomy thoughts for so early in the day – a day which promised to be warm and fine and lovely. But both Sarah and Paul, at that moment, were too busy with their own thoughts and the immediate prospects ahead to divine these emotions which all parents have when they see their fledglings about to spread their wings and fly...

They were away in good time, each astride one of the best geldings, giving them their heads for a time and pulling up now and then, breathless and excited. Sarah's eyes sparkled, and the early sun touched her hair with gold even as the rush of air, when the horses galloped, caused her cheeks to assume the soft colouring of a pale pink rose.

Soon the grey-blue line ahead, marking

the river course, changed to green, and well before ten o'clock Paul and Sarah were trotting their mounts over the road-bridge into Lariat.

Already the town was crowded. This was to be a big event; more so even than the arrival of the stage-coach; far more exciting than an ordinary wedding.

Saddle horses and rigs of all kinds were beginning to fill vacant lots. Cow-hands, lucky enough to have gotten away from ranch and range chores, sought out stores and saloons. Women contrived to get their shopping over while there was still room on the side-walks. Only the stores, saloons and deadfalls lower down would remain open today, the business section having long realized the impracticability of attempting to concentrate even on routine matters.

The babble was low as yet, but it would mount with every minute consumed and burst into an explosive roar by noon, when Kearney and his bride were due at the 'dobe church.

Paul watched the endless procession of folks engaged on chores or pleasure. The geldings were in the livery, and Paul began leading the way towards Marshal Toomis's office, the first port of call. Several people spoke to the Escorts or waved a hand. One of these was Twitchell, whose gaze moved quickly from Paul's tall figure and remained fixedly on Sarah's flushed face. Paul had the uncomfortable feeling that his sister might well be falling for the wrong man.

He took her arm, guiding her through the throng and into the marshal's office. With the door closed behind them a good deal of the racket outside was shut out.

'Glad you managed to get here before anything has a chance to pop.' Toomis grinned, glancing from Escort to his pretty sister. 'If I didn't know,' the marshal continued gallantly, 'I'd sure 'nough have had yore purty sister figgered as the bride!'

Paul grinned and glanced at Sarah, who was blushing mightily. 'I didn't realize you knew her, Marshal.'

'I don't, really,' Toomis admitted, getting to his feet and shaking their hands. 'But I seen yore sister once-twice when you brung her into town. She's like you, too, Paul. Couldn't be no mistakin' it.'

'Well,' Paul said, 'we came here first to let you know we're in town. I aim to keep Sarah off the streets as much as possible. After the wedding she'll be at Trail House–'

'Sure, I'll give Sarah a look in there every so often, though I don't reckon things'll liven up much 'till later. I'm fixin' to keep the streets as clear as possible tonight, Paul, and 'cept for the wimmen goin' to the dance I want them off the walks by sundown.'

'A kind of curfew?'

'Yep! Though we cain't force 'em to go home, but by then, as far as the wimmen is concerned, the show'll be about over after the Kearneys drive away.'

'Wedding's around noon, isn't it?'

Toomis nodded. 'We've plenty of time if you wanta take a walk round with your sister. When you got her settled in Trail House you better report back here, Paul.'

Escort nodded. 'Sarah will be going to the dance later. I'll want to see her along to Harvey's barn…'

Paul booked a room for his sister at Trail House so that she would have somewhere to wash and freshen up before evening.

They decided to get a meal early, both for the purpose of avoiding over-crowded restaurants and also because Paul might not have time to eat later on. They were amongst the first diners in the hotel's restaurant, and by the time they had finished it was a little after eleven o'clock.

Sarah selected a rocker in the hotel lobby near the open doors, while Paul made his way across the thronging street towards the office of Marshal Rich Toomis.

Crowds lined the rough path outside the 'dobe church in a solid mass of talking, laughing, jogging humanity. For the most part, sun-bonneted women with children at their trailing skirts occupied the front rows, with older kids and the menfolk behind.

At the moment Paul was quite satisfied that his sister, whose excited face and gleaming hair he could clearly see across from him, was perfectly safe.

Neither Toomis nor Paul figured there would be any trouble outside the church, if trouble there was going to be. Even that possibility was based on no more than a hunch. Toomis was not an over-imaginative man, but he had fought against many Indian uprisings and had a war-horse's ability to 'smell' trouble. He had 'smelled' it ever since he had propositioned Escort. Now, today, that premonition was stronger still, but Toomis and Escort were agreed that *if* – and it was still a big *if* – someone was going to take this chance of laying for Frank Kearney, then most likely it would happen during the drive down Main, *not* near the church.

There were several reasons for this surmise, which the marshal and Escort had gone into carefully. For one thing, there was not so much chance of an assailant getting clear of the crowds around the church by virtue of the fact that the building stood isolated.

But from Main Street a man could dive quickly down an alley or side-street to a waiting horse and get clear of town before anyone had a chance to grab a mount in the confusion.

By judicious yet casual questioning, Toomis had learned that the couple would emerge from the church, after the wedding, and that Frank would drive the buckboard down Main and pull in at the Trail House so that a couple of the Hackamore hands, riding along, could pick up Rona Jefford's valises and trunk which would be standing ready in the hotel lobby.

Toomis had learned, by questioning the hotel clerk, that Miss Jefford was not stopping off to change her costume, but was proceeding straight to Hackamore. Miss Jefford had paid her bill; everything was ready.

Now a loud burst of shouting and cheering tore the air as Rona Jefford and Frank Kearney drove up in a buckboard in a swirl of dust, scattering the kids who were playing tag. Behind the buckboard rode Jed Segal, Hackamore's present ramrod, and, ranging him, seven-eight riders.

The crowd were forced to move back a little as Kearney tooled the buckboard to the very doorway of the church. In a moment he had handed down the lovely woman who was to be his wife and was hurrying her into the comparative quiet and peace of the church. Segal, having thrown his reins to one of the punchers to hold, followed on the heels of his boss, whilst the others, still mounted, remained outside the church.

Across the path, Toomis, managing at last

to make himself seen and attract Paul's attention, jerked his head in the pre-arranged signal. That meant that Toomis would stay by the church during and after the service, to watch things there, and Paul would now wander down towards the hotel and take up a good position whilst the street was deserted. Thus, as far as two men were able to arrange such a thing, Kearney and his bride would be covered by one or other of them whilst they were in town. Add to that the fact that eight Hackamore riders were in close attendance and things should remain well under control.

But no one, perhaps not even Red Twitchell, had ever appreciated the depths of bitter hatred which lay in Ace Charro's heart and which, as always, directed itself against the man who had – however rightly – fired him.

Perhaps a man other than Charro himself would have breathed his relief that the evidence had not been sufficient for a hanging or even a formal warrant of arrest.

Kearney had been pretty sure, but he had no real proof. He did what any man in those days had the right to do with regard to an unsatisfactory rider. He fired him. And such was the half-breed's make-up that, instead of counting himself lucky and hitting the trail to start afresh some place else, had hung around, plotting and scheming to *hurt*

Kearney somehow; *kill* him if possible.

Well, thanks to Charlie Widgeon and Red Twitchell and Ace himself, it sure looked like they'd be able to hurt Hackamore all right. A pity Frank wouldn't be alive to know about the big steal. But this wedding business was too good a chance to miss.

Charro had been over the ground very carefully and he was sure nothing could come unstuck. For the past week or so he had had one of the cheaper rooms at the rear of Trail House – which had suited his purpose very well.

It was a simple matter to climb through the window and from there drop on to the sloping shed roof beneath, and then on to the ground seven-eight feet below. He had done this several times and had found it to be childishly simple. Today, his horse stood in the lot at the rear of the hotel, as it had every right to be there. A careful observer, however, might have noticed that the horse was tied closer to the hotel's side alley than usual.

And, not only was it easy to reach the ground from Ace Charro's room, but the same thing applied to the flat roof of the hotel, which jutted out no more than a couple of feet above Charro's window.

He was completely hidden, now, behind the false front looking on to Main. There was only one man on the street at the moment, and Ace Charro, peeping furtively over the lower part of the false front, thought he recognized the figure of the Escort kid. He wondered at this, feeling the first vague probe of anxiety. But almost immediately the man strolled into the saddlery across the way and became lost to Charro's sight.

CHAPTER V

Invitation to Hackamore

Right up to that moment Paul had not been certain as to which position would be best for him to take up; which spot would give him the best unrestricted view of Main, and Trail House in particular.

If he were to remain on the board-walk he would be virtually powerless to move or take any fast action in the advent of trouble. Wherever he stood, just so long as he was on the street, he ran a good chance of being caught up by the crowd, which would eventually pour down here like a torrent, and being tossed like a piece of driftwood in a fast-running swollen river.

Inside the saddlery, whose owner had left the door unlocked, Escort discovered a small flight of stairs to the rear which led upwards.

After a quick glance through the windows at the deserted street, Escort cat-footed across the shop and climbed the stairs, hardly aware why he was moving so quietly. At the top he found a room which was obviously the saddler's kitchen and bedroom in one, and which ran the entire length of the shop below.

He walked to the window and started to raise the sash as the distant clamour of voices told him that Kearney and his bride must be emerging from the church.

The window went up with no more than a few protesting squeaks, and some innate animal instinct laid sudden caution on him, so that he refrained from sticking his head and shoulders out, as he had intended.

Instead, he squatted down on his boot-heels, looking through the eighteen-inch space of open window. Involuntarily his gaze moved upstreet as the sounds of pounding hoofs and turning wheels came to his ears, even above the excited clamour of the crowd.

Kids ran down the street, scuttling out of the path of Kearney's bowling buckboard. Women scolded young offenders and men laughed and raised their voices as the whole cavalcade – buckboard, Hackamore riders and the following townsfolk – swept on to Main.

Frank Kearney, Paul could see, was pretty adept at handling the Morgans harnessed to the light vehicle.

Frank, for all that he was dressed in his best – dark corduroy jacket, low-crowned black hat, spotless linen and pearl-grey pants tucked into half-boots – would not be dissuaded from handling the reins himself. Segal had pointed out that the owner of Hackamore was 'too big,' and Frank, in his brash, boisterous way, had said something about that being damned for a tale! Did Segal figure he was too *old* to handle a span of Morgans and a damned fine filly into the bargain!

There had been no answer to that; not one that Segal would have cared to make, and, despite Kearney's sixty years, he seemed to have the strength and cool ability of a man half his age.

They drew up in front of Trail House in a cloud of dust, Kearney laughing in his boisterous fashion, hauling on the reins and glancing for approval at the girl by his side.

Paul, feeling absurdly like a peeping Tom from his hideout spot over the saddlery, caught his breath as he gazed at Rona Jefford's magnificence. *Rona Kearney,* Paul hastily corrected himself, and felt, with the sudden realization of that truth, some spark inside him flare and then die down.

She had an oyster-coloured tricorn hat with a small magenta feather and magenta veil. The beige dust coat was open to reveal

73

the rich beauty of the gown, oyster-grey, exactly matching the tiny hat atop her fair curls, and offset by the magenta ribbons and ruching at the square, low-cut neck.

Now that the crowd had more opportunity to study her, there were gusty howls of approval from the male section and twitterings from the women, some shocked, others honestly envious of Rona Kearney's regal beauty and her ability to wear such a dress.

For seconds on end Paul Escort seemed to forget where he was or for what purpose he crouched before an open window. He feasted his eyes on the lovely woman no more than twenty yards away from him – and all but failed in the task that had been set him!

Down below, two Hackamore hands were sweating to load Rona Kearney's grips and trunk into the back of the vehicle. In spite of Frank's protests about this – his assurance to send a wagon out to pick up Rona's luggage – the girl had insisted that it went with them in the buckboard. That small incident was perhaps the first real indication Frank Kearney had had that his wife possessed far too much determination and individuality to be in any way a tintype of the average woman of that period.

Frank watched the commotion with amused tolerance, chewing on an unlit cigar.

Rona had turned back on the seat from directing the loading operations and, in that infinitesimal space of time before settling her gaze ahead, her eyes lifted slightly as though magnetically drawn to that calm, steady face looking down at her from the window across the street.

And, at the moment their glances clashed and locked, Escort became aware of the slightest movement opposite him. It could have been a bird flitting across the roof in search of crumbs, or a piece of paper dislodged by a sudden swirl of wind. But when Escort tore his gaze away from that lovely upturned face he saw that it was no such innocent thing.

He glimpsed the head of the man and the rifle almost simultaneously with drawing his own gun in a smooth, liquid movement. And in a flash he recognized the narrow features of Ace Charro below the wide-brimmed hat, and divined the wicked purpose of the man.

It would be a steep angle shot to make from that roof, necessitating the would-be ambusher to show himself for a second. But it was by no means a particularly difficult shot, as the buckboard and team stood well away from the boardwalk, and Frank Kearney sat at the right-hand end of the seat *away* from the side-walk and nearest to the middle of the street.

Paul had no time to glance back at the girl,

to see the horror dawning in her eyes at sight of his gun resting on the window ledge. His brain and body were concentrated on the task of lining his sights on the figure crouched behind the false front of the hotel. Even then, Charro was showing so little of himself that unless a man on the street deliberately looked upwards for some reason, it was doubtful whether Charro would be seen at all. Even the sun did not seem to catch the rifle barrel on the roof sufficiently to throw back a gleam into anyone's eyes. The crowd, still noisy and laughing, were too absorbed in the excitement of the moment to notice anything untoward.

Paul had hesitated for a second, anxious to make absolutely certain that this was no drunken-fool practical joke. But there was nothing wavering about that rifle barrel and no chance that the man across the street had anything other than murder in his heart.

Escort, as he crouched, kneeling on one knee, was in just the right position to rest the Colt on the window ledge and draw a careful bead. A single shot rang out above the crowd's noise, and with that shot all sound became cut off as though a heavy door had been slammed effectively and abruptly shutting off the uproar.

But the silence reigned for no longer than the time it takes for a man to draw breath or a woman to scream. Ace Charro's rifle clattered from his nerveless grasp down on to the street below, scattering for a moment those gathered in the immediate vicinity.

Meanwhile, Frank Kearney had his hands full with the nearly spooked horses. Only the Hackamore owner's terrific strength kept the Morgans from bolting as Kearney sawed on the reins, forcing the horses' heads back and causing the animals to rear on hind legs through his own sheer brute strength.

Men and women were rapidly recovering from the shock. Several pointed to the form of Ace Charro, his head and shoulders just visible behind the false front above. It looked for all the world as though he were kneeling there, praying, or just regarding them sombrely with his glazed, open eyes.

They saw, too, the curl of smoke which had issued from Jo Bromley's window at the saddlery, and then, as Marshal Toomis shouldered his way through the crowd, Paul Escort appeared at the door of the saddle-shop and began walking slowly down the lane which the crowd formed for him.

A man said, 'Bigawd, Escort's done it again. Fust Jack Cotter an' now thet hombre on the roof–'

'He looks so – so gentle!' a woman ex-claimed, and a voice answered her: 'Sure! The dadblasted, gentlest gunfighter I ever seed!'

Hackamore riders were gazing wildly

around, hands on guns. Segal had drawn his, in fact, and was almost wishing he could find a target.

Kearney had the horses under control, his face red and mottled from his efforts. Rona sat poised and calm, her eyes not on her husband, but on the tranquil face of 'the gentle gunman.'

Toomis's voice boomed out. 'Good shootin' thet, Paul. Sure lucky fer Mr an' Mrs Kearney we had you on the job. Did you see who the bushwhacker was?'

Toomis peered upwards, but Charro's face, part shaded and part hidden by the false front, was difficult of positive identification now.

'It's Charro, Marshal,' Paul said quietly. 'I guess maybe he had a grudge of some kind against Mr Kearney here. He sure enough had his sights lined on your pearl button, Mr Kearney.' Paul smiled.

'By God, kid. Who *are* you? I reckon we owe you plenty for what you did. Ace Charro, eh? Jest the kind o' dirty, sneakin' trick he'd figure on playin'.'

'This is Paul Escort,' Toomis said. 'Deputy marshal for a day–'

'Escort, huh? Ain't that the name o' them hoss ranchers south of the river?'

Paul looked towards Toomis, who was directing two men to go round back and fetch down Charro's lodged body. The

78

marshal had already taken charge of the unfired Winchester and now handed it to Paul, a grin on his seamed face.

'Spoils of war, son. Seems like you got best rights to this. It's a good one, too!' Paul took the carbine, appreciating the balanced weight of it as he held it at the breech.

'My folks run a horse ranch, Mr Kearney, that's right. You ever need some good army-standard geldings, let me know.' His glance slid from Kearney's face to the girl's. She was watching him carefully, a soft light in her eyes.

Paul turned on his heel, but Kearney's bull-like roar stopped him in his tracks.

'Hold et, Escort. You ain't walkin' out on us like that. Come along to the ranch and enjoy yourself for a spell. 'Sides which, mebbe I'd like to talk some more about those geldings you breed!'

Paul flushed with pleasure.

'That's handsome of you, Mr Kearney, invitin' me out like that, but I guess I'm being paid to stay here and help out the marshal today. Also I have my sister with–'

'Don't stand there arguin', Escort,' Kearney said, with a rough kindness under the bombast, 'bring your sister along too. As for helpin' the marshal, my range-boss'll fix that. Jed!' Kearney called, 'deputize a man to replace Escort for the remainder of the day. I'll pay him double wages for a week.'

He lifted the reins, confident that everything would be done as he had commanded.

'See you an' your sister later,' Kearney growled, 'an' thanks again!'

The crowd, chattering again now, broke as the buckboard got under way, Segal and the others following close behind. A Hackamore man remained behind, grinning broadly. Just for staying in town the rest of the day he'd draw double wages for a week. What a difference marriage made to a man, he reflected! Or perhaps it was really because that hombre Escort had saved Frank's life!

It had been Escort's remark to Kearney about his sister which had jerked Paul up sharply with a guilty start. True enough he was helping Toomis as a deputy, but that was a poor excuse for him to forget that Sarah had first claim to his protection.

Nevertheless, when Paul had glimpsed his sister's figure in the throng outside the church, he had felt that she was safe enough surrounded by a mixed crowd in good humour.

After that, events had moved too quickly for Paul to indulge in any kind of speculative thoughts, except, he reminded himself guiltily, concerning Rona Kearney!

Now, with Hackamore riding from town and the mass of people breaking up into smaller groups, Paul's anxious glance searched for the familiar face and form of his sister.

He found her, not far away, her eyes glowing with excitement, for although she had not *seen* her brother shoot the ambusher, the story was being tossed from one chattering group to another.

She came walking towards him almost at the same time that he glimpsed her shining face. He caught her by the arm and led her on to the walk where Toomis and the Hackamore hand stood grinning at them.

'You got a right smart brother there, Miz Sarah,' the marshal said. 'Has he told you he's runnin' out on me?'

Sarah's eyes widened. 'Why, Marshal, I don't understand. Paul hasn't had time to tell me anything yet, but I'm sure he wouldn't run out on you–'

Toomis laughed. 'Tell her, Paul,' he ordered.

Escort smiled at the two men and gave his sister an oblique, measuring glance.

'If it's all right with Marshal Toomis,' he told her, 'we've been invited to Hackamore for the rest of the day. Seems like Mr Kearney's plumb grateful for something or other–'

'You've done gone an' made yoreself a friend in the boss, Escort,' the Hackamore rider opined. 'My name's Grady – Jim Grady – an' I'm shore glad to make your acquaintance.' He extended a work-worn, calloused hand and winced slightly as Paul returned the grip.

'You pack a wallop in more ways than one, mister,' Grady grinned. 'You know how to get out to Hackamore, I guess?'

Paul grinned. 'Never been there, but I guess we could follow the dust cloud.'

Grady nodded. 'A half-mile out of town you'll find a trail branching off to the right from the stage road. Another six miles you'll see the ranch.'

'Better all come into the office,' Toomis suggested, suiting the action to the word.

The three of them sat while the marshal rummaged for and found a handful of silver dollars. He counted out ten, and Escort said, 'No, Marshal. I haven't earned my full pay...'

'The hell you ain't,' Toomis growled. 'If Kearney knew you rated him no higher than ten bucks, he'd nail yore hide to a post!'

'Don't worry on my account, Escort,' Jim Grady drawled. 'You heard Frank's offer an' he never backs down.'

Paul took the money reluctantly. Quite honestly he could not see how he had earned a day's pay for an hour's work.

Outside he grinned and thrust five dollars into Sarah's hand. 'That's to make up for missing the dance tonight, kid. Buy a hat or some gee-gaw that takes your fancy–'

'Thanks a lot, Paul. I reckon yore a good guy even though you are my brother!' She laughed and dropped the silver coins into her skirt pocket.

'I ain't spending it now,' she said, and added cryptically, 'I gotta reason fer savin', I guess–'

Escort smiled, shepherding her across the street and down towards the livery.

Within the space of fifteen minutes they were riding at an easy pace out of town. Toomis didn't expect any trouble worse than a few drunken brawls later on, and Jim Grady was along to give him a hand.

Thus, Paul rode with a clear mind and a clear conscience except when the image of a golden-haired, steady-eyed girl came between his eyes and the undulating grassland. Then he felt as guilty as all hell!

Sarah, riding at his stirrup, noticed the colour tinge his dark cheeks.

'She *is* beautiful, isn't she, Paul?'

Escort's flush deepened still further in his confusion.

'Oh, I didn't see everything, Paul,' Sarah laughed, 'but I *did* see the way you looked at Rona Kearney after the shooting, and I cain't say I blame you–'

'It's nothing like that, Sary,' Paul managed at last. 'She is pretty, I guess–'

'Pretty!' Sarah scoffed. 'That's not the word I'd use. *I'm* pretty, mebbe,' she said

83

ingenuously. 'Rona Kearney's downright lovely, like – like a goddess–'

'Quit this fool talk, Sarah, will you? She means nothing to me and it's a shameful thing to – to think of a newly married woman like that–'

'So you *do* think of her – like *that?*' Sarah said wickedly and spurred the gelding into a long run before her brother could reply...

From the top of a low knoll they gazed down at the headquarters of Hackamore nestling in a broad, saucer-shaped hollow.

A stream, bordered with cottonwoods and willows, meandered through the buffalo grass. A windbreak of closely planted trees protected the ranch-house on the winter side.

The house itself was wood, two-storied and galleried, with a wood shingle roof and two stone chimneys. It was painted white and brown and was just about the biggest house or building either of the Escorts had ever seen. Beyond the house were all the outbuildings and fixtures of a vast, well-run cattle ranch: corrals, stables, barns, bunk-house, blacksmith shop, windmill, hay ricks. Now the yard was cluttered with surreys, democrats, spring wagons and saddle-horses of the many guests whom Kearney had invited. Everybody who was anybody in the entire valley – and a few who weren't – were there, laughing, talking and making great inroads into the magnificent board and the vast quantities of liquor which Kearney had laid on.

As soon as they had entered the yard, their mounts had been taken by a wrangler and Jed Segal had appeared at the door beckoning them on inside.

The huge living room was crowded almost to overflowing. Flunkeys, imported specially for the reception, scurried every which way, refilling plates and dishes on the buffet table as soon as they were approaching empty.

Glasses clinked and wine flowed freely, and in the midst of it all Frank, glass in hand and cigar in mouth, received the congratulations of all.

Rona had already changed into a gown of such surpassing loveliness that few, if any, of the men there could keep their eyes off her for more than a few moments at a time.

It was a black gown of rustling taffeta, bare at the shoulders, with a tight-fitting corsage sufficiently *décolleté* to reveal more than a suggestion of softly rounded bosom. Smoke-grey tulle softened the neckline, caught between the breasts by a diamond brooch of fabulous brilliance, matched only by the diamonds shining in the eyes; eyes, Paul realized suddenly, which were the colour of rain-washed birch-bark.

Frank came shouldering his way through the press, unmindful of spilled glasses in his eagerness to greet the new arrivals.

He pumped Paul's hand enthusiastically and slanted his gaze down to Sarah's up-turned face with something more than paternal appreciation.

'I don't reckon you two've been intro-duced to my wife,' he boomed, turning his thick red neck in the direction of Rona. 'Hey, Rona!' he bawled, 'come here a min-ute an' meet Escort an' his sister.'

Rona smiled and moved gracefully through the crowd, achieving the same result that Frank had done but without any of the belligerence.

She stood before them, a gracious, almost regal-looking figure, holding out her hand in welcome, and Paul found himself wondering how it was that this beautiful woman had come to marry Frank Kearney. He won-dered, Did she love him? and felt strangely disturbed by these thoughts.

Her voice was low and husky, just as Paul would have expected.

'We haven't had time to thank you properly for saving Frank's life, Mr Escort,' she said softly. 'I guess if it had not been for you–'

'Rona would sure have bin a bride an' a widow within an hour!' Kearney inter-rupted heartily.

Paul stood amazed. It seemed not to worry Frank Kearney at all, this narrow brush with death, and all on his wedding day. Perhaps, he thought, Kearney had seen death too often for it to move him!

'And this is Sarah, Paul's sister,' Rona continued as though Frank had not spoken. 'Welcome to Hackamore, the both of you. Our house is yours!' She spoke in American, even the last four words, yet Escort had the feeling that she had been *thinking* in Spanish. *My house is yours* – the most hospitable remark that a Spanish-American could make and a compliment which always came from the depths of the heart.

Paul Escort felt that only now was he beginning to touch the fringe of life, for the first time in his twenty years.

He looked around for his sister and spotted her in the midst of a group of young cowboys, all on their best behaviour. He grinned. He supposed he didn't have to worry over Sarah. Frank's voice was booming in his ear.

'Come into my office, Escort. I want to get one or two things straightened out.'

Paul followed Hackamore's owner through the press of people, out of the room and along the hall to a door farther down. He had no idea what it was that Frank Kearney wanted to get 'straightened out' – but he would soon know…

CHAPTER VI

A Job at Hackamore

For all that Kearney's office was essentially a man's room, with harness leathers, saddles, guns scattered about in wild disorder, it nevertheless bore every evidence that, like the rest of the place, expense had not been spared.

Kearney sat at a polished walnut desk whose beauty was not entirely camouflaged by the profusion of papers and books on its top. There were deep leather chairs, which few, even wealthy ranchers, would have considered worth freighting in from distant towns.

Against one wall stood a walnut chiffonier with a fitted mirror. On top stood an array of liquors in cut-glass decanters, as well as bottles, the like of which Paul had never seen before in a private residence.

Kearney waved a hand towards the chiffonier. 'Pour yourself a drink, Escort, and one for me. Whiskey's in the decanter nearest to you.'

Paul sloshed a modest two fingers into a glass for himself and half-filled one for

Kearney, carrying them across the room and setting them on the desk.

He selected a rawhide-bottomed chair and looked at Hackamore's owner with calm patience.

Kearney sipped his drink, smacked his lips and then grinned, selecting a cigar and pushing the humidor towards Paul.

'I'd rather smoke a *cigarrito,* if you won't mind, Mr Kearney.'

'Go ahead, son,' Frank invited, and went on, 'Apart from the fact that you saved my life, Escort, I like you! You must be wondering why I brought you in here, yet you sit there with a face as wooden as a damned Injun. Aren't you even curious?'

Paul smiled. 'I guess you'll tell me whatever it is you want me to know, all in good time.'

Kearney blew cigar smoke. 'I'm a lucky hombre,' he said. 'A lovely wife and an unsuccessful murder attempt on the same day! Now, Escort. I'm not one to waste overmuch time in talking. I'd like you to ride for Hackamore. No! Wait–' He held up his cigar hand peremptorily as Paul made to protest.

'Let me finish,' Kearney growled. 'I kin see straight off you know cattle as well as hosses. You got the stamp on you. Moreover, you'd earn your pay even if you never chased or branded a steer–'

'How?'

Kearney indicated the Colt in the other's holster.

'Yore gun,' he said.

'Are you trying to hire a gun hand–?'

'Hell, Escort! I don't have to draw a picture for you, do I? Like most big ranchers, I got enemies. One less now, thanks to you, but there's others. I got a wife, too, an' I want to live long enough to enjoy marriage, a home–'

He broke off, as though conscious of having revealed a part of what lay beneath his tough exterior.

'*All* Hackamore hands can use their guns, and if by that you'd tag them as gunfighters – well, then, by God, they are–'

'I'm sorry,' Paul said quietly. 'I didn't quite get what was in your mind. I wouldn't be any man's gunsel, not for a fortune. I've killed a man today; it was something that I had to do. I didn't want to. Beyond that, there were three Apaches a few years back. They were killed as Ace Charro was killed today, to save lives, to attempt the establishment of some law and order.'

Kearney stared. This kid had it all figured out – the ethical and moral side of it all. He didn't relish killing, yet he drew fast, by all accounts, and shot with a cool and deadly accuracy.

'I've got no one special in mind I want salivatin',' Kearney said with brittle humour, 'but a man has to take care of himself – and his family. There's been talk in the bunk-house, too, of rustling. Not much, but a little. That's why I make sure my night-hawks and round-up crews can handle guns as well as ropes. They get well paid for their trouble. That's why I'm offering *you* a job–'

Paul said, 'Well, Mr Kearney, I'm sure glad I had you pegged wrongly and I'm sorry I took your meaning the wrong way. But I guess I couldn't ride for Hackamore, or anyone. You see–'

'So you haveta do most of the chores at home and look after the horses,' Kearney said shrewdly. 'And by the looks of you I'd figure you do the lion's share. You cain't take a riding job with Hackamore because how would your folks get along without you? Is that it?'

Paul flushed. 'Well–' He didn't quite know how to go on. Some things were pretty difficult to explain.

But Kearney was writing something in a book, as far as Escort could see, and with a final flourish of the pen he blotted the paper and tore it down the perforated line. He handed it over, and Paul saw, with amaze-ment, that it was a cheque made payable to his mother *for a thousand dollars!*

'You can deposit that cheque in Lariat's bank as soon as you like, Escort. That should leave your mind easy about your folk. They'll have enough *dinero* to hire help if they should want, in place of you. Besides that, there's no reason why you shouldn't ride over once a week and give them a hand. You can look on that cheque as a small token of my appreciation for what you did today.'

Paul thought, *I wouldn't want this for myself, but father and mother and Sary–*

Slowly Escort folded the coloured slip of paper and placed it carefully in a shirt pocket.

'I think you're being mighty generous, sir, not only to me but my folks as well. Why did you make out this cheque to my mother?'

Kearney coughed. 'I heard tell – well, the fact of the matter is, I figured mebbe your mother might–'

'–Make it last a little longer?' Paul finished with a meagre smile. 'I guess you're right. When do I report for work?'

'See Jed Segal tonight, after this shindig is over, and tell him you're on the pay-roll. He'll start you in tomorrow morning. Oh, and about wages. Forty a month all found, bonuses for extra work and a percentage on the cattle we sell after the trail drives. You'll find Hackamore looks after its men even though Ace Charro didn't seem to figure it that way.' He rose from the chair, a big man and nearly as tall and broad as Escort.

'I must get back to my wife and the guests. You wander around, Escort, and eat when you want. They's plenty of everything. Oh, I'd almost forgotten your sister. You'll want to ride back with her later?'

'I'll give the cheque to Toomis at the same time,' Paul said, 'then he can deposit it for me at nine o'clock tomorrow.'

Frank nodded, leading the way out of the office and back to where the guests still milled around the groaning food table, talking, eating, drinking. For a long time afterwards folk would talk about the Kearney wedding and reception.

The Yucca saloon was as packed as any other place in town, but Red Twitchell and Jack Cotter shoved their way through the crowd, oblivious to the half-muttered angry protests.

Twitchell knocked on the door and, scarcely waiting for the invitation to come in, entered quickly with Cotter hard on his heels.

As the door closed, the noise from the saloon became considerably muted. Charlie Widgeon looked up from his desk and then waddled across to the table on which stood the inevitable bottle and three glasses.

He waved a pudgy, impatient hand for the others to be seated and said softly, 'Tell me about that stupid fool, Red!'

Twitchell pushed back his hat and lit a *cigarrito*. His face was set in unusually sober lines. There was no vestige of a smile even on the broad mouth.

He said, exhaling smoke, 'The goddam fool, trying to settle a personal grudge at a time like this! I figgered Ace had more brains–'

'Never mind the recriminations, Red; let's have *yore* version.'

Twitchell shrugged. 'I probably know little more than you do. But it seems that Toomis musta had some kind of an idea that something would happen, though I don't reckon he had it figgered that Charro would try and bushwhack Frank Kearney in front of nearly a thousand people.'

Widgeon nodded. 'How did the kid come to play such a big part?'

'Far as I could find out, later,' Twitchell said, 'Toomis had picked him as a kind of semi-official deputy, jest for the day. Whose idea it was for Escort to watch from over the saddle shop, I don't know, but he sure enough was in a swell position to line his sights on Charro across the street. I guess Ace never knew what took him square in the forehead.'

'That's shootin',' Charlie said softly.

'He's not only as good as Bonney with a gun,' Cotter said with feeling, 'but he's got the strength of a dozen wild cats–'

'I said before not to underestimate him,' Widgeon reminded Red. 'Mebbe *I'd* best stop calling him "the Kid"!'

'He's gotta new handle now,' Twitchell sneered. 'Some folks is callin' him "the Gentle Gunman"–'

'And they're not so far wrong, Red, from what I've heard. But what I wanta know is *did you get to the body first?*'

Twitchell nodded. 'Fust thing I thought of, Charlie. I went through his pockets in five seconds flat, before the marshal sent men up to haul him down. He hadn't a thing on him that would point a finger in any direction!'

'First time he's showed sense,' Widgeon said coldly. 'That's all right, then. Charro had already outgrown his usefulness. He's told us what Hackamore's going to do – and when.'

Cotter didn't quite like the way Widgeon spoke, but he said nothing. He poured himself a modest drink and took half of it in a gulp.

'There's something else, Charlie,' Twitchell said presently, 'which you may not know. I was close enough to Kearney and Escort, after the shootin', to hear Frank invite Escort and his sister to the ranch for the rest of the day.'

'Any particular significance?' Widgeon said. He had his own ideas with regard to this piece of information, but he wanted to find out what sense, if any, it made to Twitchell.

Red said slowly, 'Could be that Frank will be feelin' grateful enough to offer Escort a job – a good one – in recognition of savin' his life *and because Frank's nobody's fool!*'

'Meanin'?'

'Meaning that Frank knows a good bet when he sees one. This Escort hombre would be worth a hundred a month to someone like Kearney, just for his gun alone–'

'Maybe,' Widgeon agreed. But he wasn't going to give Red the satisfaction of knowing that was exactly the way *he* had worked this out. Supposition only, at the moment, but they would soon find out whether their ideas were right.

And if Escort *were* to be offered a riding job at Hackamore, it would automatically remove one big barrier which might have jeopardized the execution of Red's plan.

Charlie Widgeon smiled as he thought about this. 'Now that we know where we stand with the Escorts,' he said, 'it's goin' to make your job easier, Red, if Paul Escort *is* offered a job at Hackamore!'

Twitchell's face relaxed for the first time since he had entered Charlie's office. He hadn't been relishing this interview, but apparently Widgeon was attaching no blame to *him* for Charro's blunder, which, after all, had cost them nothing – only Charro's death – which Widgeon was beginning to write down as an asset rather than a loss.

Twitchell's slow smile spread almost to his green eyes. 'We'll pretty soon hear in town if Frank's goin' to take the kid on his pay-roll. If he *does*, then, like you say, Charlie, we won't have no trouble at the Escort place. I don't mind admittin' I was a mite worried about Paul bein' there, him so handy with his gun–'

Widgeon nodded approvingly. 'It's smart to admit when you're worried about someone, Red. It's more likely you can find a solution to the problem if you can appreciate your adversary's ability. Only fools think the man isn't born who can lick 'em. What about the cattle, Red?'

'Jack's been doin' a heap of ridin'. Say yore piece, Jack.'

Cotter, too had felt a little apprehensive about this interview with the Yucca saloon owner. This was the first time Cotter had seen Widgeon since the episode with Corinne and Escort on the board-walk outside. He had been wondering whether Corinne had talked or if the news had gotten around that he, Jack Cotter, had mauled the girl and had, in turn, been mauled by young Escort. But Corinne, in fact, had not recounted the episode to Widgeon, and thus bar-keep and houseman inside the Yucca had been careful to steer clear of the subject when the owner made his rounds of the bar and tables. If Widgeon was to hear about it, then let it come from the girl's own lips.

But Jack Cotter was finding Charlie quite amiable, as Red had done, and, with his confidence restored, he elaborated on the movements of Hackamore stuff and their riders.

'Charro was right,' Cotter finished, 'if he told you they was to haze a herd down to the dog-leg section near the Escort place. Another week, less mebbe, the rate they're workin', oughta see the right-sized herd there ready fer movin'.'

'Well, Charlie,' Red said, 'it looks like you're goin' to save yourself a couple of thousand over Escort's place. It would've been a shame,' he grinned, 'if you'd hadta pay that *dinero* jest so's we could burn the place down!'

'You're quite sure it *is* necessary, Red? Oh, I ain't worried about *them*. I'm only concerned that Toomis and everyone in town'll lap up the story it's Apache work!'

'Even if Paul's away,' Red replied slowly, 'it still wouldn't make it safe for us to haze a thousand head at night, past the Escort place an' down to the border. The old man or his wife'd likely hear the ruckus an' come out to investigate. They bin here long enough to know Hackamore don't drive its herds *south* along the edge of the desert, nor at night!'

Charlie nodded, placed both fat hands on

the table and levered himself into an upright position. The interview was over. All he said now was, 'Watch your step, Red, an' make sure the kid's well away from the place before you burn it down. If Paul don't swallow the story,' he added softly, 'it's shore goin' to be too bad for him!'

The two men nodded and stepped through the doorway into the full, raucous activity of the saloon...

Corinne, acting croupier at the roulette table, watched them covertly. Of late, Red had been too damnably busy to see much of her. When he did he spoke lightly, but vaguely, of business. Yet, she thought bitterly, all he does is to closet himself with Charlie. And tonight he'd brought along the hateful Cotter, presumably to fill the boots of the dead Ace Charro— Hastily she returned her attention to the job in hand, but later, when a houseman relieved her for supper, Corinne ran upstairs to her room and sat on the bed, her mind probing at things. Things such as the time Charlie spent in his back office often with men like Red, Cotter and the like.

Corinne was not a fool. She knew that Red did no obvious work and yet could ride a fine horse and dress well and have money in his pockets. She had never enquired too closely into the source of his gold, never thought much about it until now. But these repeated conferences were giving her cause now to start in considering one or two angles.

Several times last week, Red and Ace Charro had gone through to talk with Charlie Widgeon and had remained in the office an hour or more each time. Even when they had emerged Red had smilingly brushed her off with his vague talk of business.

Now, today, Charro had been shot and killed by Paul Escort – Corrine's face softened as she thought of Paul and how gently, and without fuss, he had saved her from the undesirable attentions of Cotter.

She wondered suddenly what Red would say and do if she told him about Cotter getting fresh. She had the uneasy feeling that Mr Twitchell would brush it aside in his characteristic fashion and do precisely nothing about it, particularly as it seemed that Jack Cotter was now a 'business associate.'

Corinne reached for a Bull Durham sack and papers lying on the dressing table and rolled a quirly. When it was alight she continued to explore the train of thought which had been set in motion by the appearance of Red and Cotter tonight.

Ace Charro, she recalled now, had been Frank Kearney's range-boss, way back. But some suspicion had fallen on him; what was it? She racked her brains and remembered that Kearney had as good as accused his ramrod of rustling and being in cahoots with owlhoots.

What if Red were an outlaw? She wondered suddenly and felt sick at the thought, not because she had any over-high moral values regarding those outside the law, but because she had come to regard Red as her means of escape from the hellish life here in Lariat.

Though Corinne was no saint, she was certainly not promiscuous, as many of the women in town whispered and believed. She had her own moral code, such as it was, and that meant she was strictly a one-man woman. She belonged to Red Twitchell and no one else.

Red, with his disarming ways and his expensive presents, his casual talk of far-away places, had captured her easily, too easily perhaps. He had spoken more than once of taking her away from Lariat and the surrounding country, once he had made a big enough stake. He had even hinted at marriage and had, with little effort, painted a picture which for Corinne had possessed the magic and beauty of a wonderful dream...

Now ... she was not quite so sure. Red was mixed up in something. Charro had been killed trying to get Frank Kearney. Maybe Red would be next in line, and oddly the thought came to the girl that it would be by the hand of Paul Escort rather than through

Toomis or the sheriff at the county seat.

Thinking of Escort again, and this time in connection with violence, Corinne reflected back, not for the first time, on what Paul had told her concerning Twitchell, in the Yucca, after Paul's handling of Cotter. Red was making an offer for the Escort place, Paul Escort had said, and again the girl speculated as to where Twitchell's money came from. He had lost a thousand dollars in the all-night game at the saloon a few weeks back and now here he was offering to *buy* the Escort ranch!

Was there any significance, Corinne wondered, in the frequent visits Red made to Charlie Widgeon's office? If so, it sure looked like Charlie was up to his neck in something as well as Red. *But why should they want a broken-down horse-ranch on the edge of the desert?* It didn't seem to make any sense at all.

Corinne stubbed out the quirly, glancing at the small pocket watch on her dressing table and realizing that she had about fifteen minutes in which to eat, before going back to the roulette wheel. But somehow, tonight, she didn't feel like eating; a drink down in the saloon would suffice. She continued to sit for a while, examining her thoughts, and every fresh idea which came into her mind seemed to open up the possibility of a dark, perhaps hopeless future.

For a moment she toyed with the idea of making a play for Paul Escort, but almost at once she dismissed such a scheme. She had a strange respect for that tranquil young man; she knew he was not the kind to be bought either with promises or money. He would always do what he felt was the *right* thing. A weird philosophy, Corinne thought, yet perversely she admired him all the more.

No! If Red were involved in trouble there was no one else she could turn to and still cling to what shreds of self-respect remained. There would be two alternatives open to her. She could either stay on at the Yucca until her good looks, and therefore her usefulness, were gone, or she could set out on her own, with the money she had saved, and try to start afresh.

She shuddered at the bleak prospects ahead, realizing for the first time the extent to which she had been living in a fool's paradise.

With a sigh, partly of resignation and partly of desperation, she arose and walked downstairs towards the noisy, smoke-laden saloon...

CHAPTER VII

A Bride Sleeps Alone

The moon was silvering the range with its clear light as Paul and Sarah rode the rough trail back to town. Both of their young hearts were high, for it seemed that fortune, at long last, was beginning to smile on the Escort name.

In Paul's pocket reposed the one-thousand-dollars' cheque which Kearney had shrewdly made out to Mrs Martha Escort and which Paul would hand to the marshal.

Toomis, he knew, would be willing to present it to the bank first thing in the morning, and, as soon as Martha had been told about it, she could drive into town, leave a specimen signature with the bank and draw on the money when and how she liked. Paul smiled in the night, knowing that his mother would probably not touch a cent herself until all debts had been paid...

'I don't know when I've had such a wonderful day, Paul,' Sarah exclaimed presently. 'I'm sure glad we didn't go to the dance after all, in that stuffy barn, dancin' with rough men an' cheeky kids pretendin' they're men!'

She sighed happily. 'The Kearneys is real *quality*, Paul, and all those nice cowboys, Hackamore, Bart Reed's BR6, Mr an' Mrs Hogan of the Diamond H – oh, all of them. And the food, Paul. My! I don't know when I've eaten so many slices of layer cake–'

Paul laughed. 'Much more of that, Sary, an' you'll be gettin' so fat you'll have to go in through the door sideways.'

'Do you suppose ma'll let me buy a new dress outa that money Mr Kearney gave you?' Sarah asked, ignoring her brother's quip. 'Mebbe if you was to–'

'I'll see what I can do to persuade her,' Paul grinned. 'There's Lariat ahead.' He pointed to the twinkling lights beyond the fork in the road. 'Now I've got to see Marshal Toomis and then we'll be on our way.'

'You ain't ridin' back all the way to Hackamore tonight, are you?'

'I was going to,' Paul replied, 'but mebbe I'll sleep in the stable again and start out right early tomorrow morning.'

'I reckon I'd be all right on my own, Paul, was you figgerin' to get back to Hackamore tonight; I know the trail blindfold.'

'Sure you know the trail, Sary,' her brother said, 'but you're not riding it alone, and at night.'

Shortly they clattered into town and drew up outside the marshal's office. Lariat's celebrations were in full swing. It was only nine o'clock; plenty of time as yet for Marshal Toomis to fill up his cells with drunken roysterers!

They swung out of saddles and tied the horses, just as the distant rataplan of racing hoofs slammed against their ears from the night range.

'Some is sure in a hurry to get here,' Paul said, pausing with one foot on the walk.

They waited as though by tacit consent; other folk, men mostly, stopped in their tracks to listen to the sounds of the fast-approaching rider.

In a few minutes he came into view, a dimly discernible shape at first, crouched low in the saddle and thundering along Main, sawing on reins now as he hit town with all the violence of a man riding for his life.

He pulled up a bare five yards from where the Escorts stood, narrowing his eyes against some of the brighter lights. Escort suddenly wondered whether any Apaches were out.

The man saw Escort's tall shape and called out in a husky voice, 'Where's the marshal's office, mister?'

'Right here, stranger,' Paul said, glancing with concern at the lathered, trembling beast. 'We were just going in–'

The man nodded and slid from leather, tossing reins over the hitch rack. His face was runnelled with sweat and trail dust and, as though he owed them some explanation, he said, 'Come all the way from the county seat. Urgent business for the marshal.'

Paul nodded, catching Sarah by the arm and leading the way to the door, which had now opened to reveal the figure of Toomis himself.

'What's all the ruckus?' he demanded. Then, seeing the Escorts in the lead, he grinned and waved the trio inside the lamplit office.

He gazed questioningly from face to face and, noticing the man's deputy badge, recognition came to him.

'Say, you're Deputy Sheriff Frank Locke, aren't you–?'

The man nodded and wiped his streaked face with the bandana at his neck. He sank into a chair, and Toomis, producing a half-filled pint bottle from his desk, sloshed some of the amber liquid into a glass and passed it across to Locke.

The deputy nodded his thanks and drained the contents, but his voice was still as husky when he spoke.

'It ain't Injuns, if that's what you folks is thinkin',' he grinned, including Paul and Sarah in his talk.

'They got Jesse Evans, Marshal; leastways, they *figger* it's Evans, an' Sheriff Commart's daid scared that Evans' sidekick, Bonney, is gettin' set to spring him some way or another. That is,' Frank Locke concluded, 'if the guy they caught *is* Evans—'

Toomis, tugging at his moustaches, stared wide-eyed.

'*Bonney?*' he rasped. 'You mean Billy the Kid?'

Frank Locke nodded. 'The two on 'em's wanted most every territory fer hoss-stealin' an' killing, but while we got likenesses of Billy, we ain't got no means of identifyin' Evans, *except through Frank Kearney of Hackamore!*'

At the marshal's hand-wave, Paul and Sarah sat down and Toomis returned his attention to the deputy from the county seat.

'Kearney?' he rasped. 'How in Hades does he set in on this thing?' And then, remembering an incident some time back, just before Ace Charro had been fired, Toomis added, 'Wait, though, wasn't there an owl-hoot named Evans way back and Kearney an' his riders caught him? The man escaped before they got him to the county seat as I recollect.'

Locke nodded. 'There ain't much wrong with your memory, Marshal. That's more or less what happened. But it was night-time and descriptions of Jesse Evans are still purty vague. Only Kearney had a real good look at him, because before the stage which was bringing Jesse to the courthouse got more'n half-way it was held up an' Evans snatched an' whisked away on a fast horse. It was Bonney, of course, who effected the rescue.

'Now we figger we got Evans but we gotta have someone to identify him an' it's urgent. They's goin' to rush the hearin' through tomorrow morning; the sheriff's hopin' the court'll send Jesse to the pen before Billy can try out any of his tricks. That's why I rode a couple of hosses to their knees gettin' here!'

'My Gawd,' Toomis said slowly, 'beggin' yore pardon, Miss Sary. This,' he continued, turning to Lock, 'is Frank Kearney's weddin' night. He jest done got himself hitched only today. You cain't drag the man from his home *tonight,* Frank!'

Locke reached for his makings and rolled a brown-paper cigarette. He blew smoke, and now, tardily, Toomis produced cups and lifted the coffee pot from the still-warm stove.

Jim Grady, the Hackamore rider, pushed open the door and stood glancing at the others doubtfully. He said, addressing Toomis, 'Everythin's all right, so far, Marshal. Every deadfall's sure makin' a heap o' noise, but I don't figger we're goin' to have any serious trouble. I reckon the shootin' today has made most o' the trouble-makers a mite thoughtful.'

Toomis nodded his agreement and introduced Grady to the deputy sheriff, explaining briefly the purpose of Frank Locke's breakneck ride.

Grady looked shocked. '*I* wouldn't like to be the guy who's gonna break the news to Frank about this–'

'Looks like you *will* be, Jim,' Toomis grinned. 'Leastways you'll haveta ride out to Hackamore *pronto* an' bring Kearney in here. After that Frank Locke here kin take over–'

'Me?' Grady's tone was horrified. 'Now wait a minute, Marshal. I only took this job for–'

'It's nothing to do with helping me out today, Jim,' Rich Toomis said patiently. 'I just gotta have a rider to take a message. If you like we'll write it down on paper. All you gotta do then is ride fast to the ranch, give the note to Frank an' wait for him.'

'I'd do it for you, Grady, willingly,' Paul put in, 'but we only stopped by here on our way home to the ranch. We got nearly thirty miles to travel tonight, me and my sister–'

Grady suddenly realized that he had been standing there with his hat on the whole time. Now he snatched the weather-stained Stetson from his sandy hair and grinned at Sarah, finally transferring his gaze to Toomis.

'Wal,' he said doubtfully, 'the way you put it, Marshal, it sure don't sound so bad. But if Frank don't come I ain't got any real authority to brung him in. Hell-an'-be-merry, I jest *work* for him!'

'There won't be any trouble, Grady,' Frank Locke opined. 'If there is, why, then I reckon I'll haveta ride out there me own self an' drag him in. But right now I could use a shave an' a meal. We'll give you a note, Grady, an' you needn't say anythin' to yore boss. This is law business an' plenty important to the county sheriff. Kearney'll haveta ride back with me tonight, so we arrive by the mornin' when the hearin's fixed for. He kin take the stage at midday and be back here in town by tomorrow night...'

And while the Escorts, brother and sister, were riding the trail south to home, Jim Grady was burning leather northwards towards Hackamore. He still didn't feel too good about this chore he had to do, but he tried to console himself with the thought that he was only a messenger detailed by the law, like a posse-man might be. He was mighty glad that Deputy Sheriff Locke had written the note to Kearney, and now all Jim Grady would have to do would be to deliver it to Frank and then stand well clear of the inevitable explosion...

He clattered into the yard, mildly surprised to notice that one-two buggies and saddle horses were still there. Evidently not all the guests had departed, and this discovery gave Grady a feeling of relief.

One of the hands came out from the shadows of the bunkhouse and called out, and Grady answered the challenge, identifying himself to Crick Rowland.

'Frank still up?' Grady asked anxiously as Rowland came up alongside.

'Sure he is,' Crick said, puzzled by the question. 'He ain't likely to turn in yet, even if it *is* his weddin' night.' He grinned. 'Anyways, Bart Reed an' his outfit's still here an' one-two other guests. Why, Jim, what's on your mind?'

Grady said, 'They want Frank up at the county seat an' identify Jesse Evans, Billy the Kid's sidekick. We gotta deputy sheriff down an' he's waitin' in town now to take Frank back tonight.'

'Gawd!' Rowland breathed. 'Don't that beat all hell, an' the boss only married today!'

'It shore ain't no joshin' matter, Crick,' Jim Grady said worriedly. 'I'd better get on in an' get it over with.'

'Mebbe I'd best saddle up Frank's chestnut, or do you figger that's kinda preemature?'

Grady was too anxious about the whole thing to join in Crick Rowland's following laughter.

He walked slowly but steadily towards the galleried house, ascended the steps and opened the screen door through which lamplight was streaming.

He passed into the living room, unbuttoning the pocket in which reposed Frank Locke's note. There were up to a dozen folks talking, smoking and drinking, and in the midst Frank stood with a cigar in one hand and his free arm encircling the slim waist of his wife.

Even to Jim Grady, Rona Kearney was beginning to look tired and drawn.

Frank looked up then and shouted, 'Hell, Jim, glad you got back before all the liquor's been drunk. Pour yourself a stiff one.' He gestured with his cigar to the buffet table, on which stood the sad remnants of the feast.

Grady hesitated a moment. But he felt he needed a drink, so he poured out a modest three fingers and downed it quickly, contriving to get close enough to whisper in Kearney's ear, 'I gotta see you privately, boss, for a few minutes. It's law business–'

'Let it wait,' Frank grinned. 'There ain't any business, law or otherwise, that's got a right to interfere with things at a time like this. I–'

Jim thrust the scrap of paper in front of the Hackamore owner. He knew it was useless to argue with Frank or to pursue further the question of a private session. Frank might as well know the truth right here and now; the sooner the better.

Bart Reed and his wife, as also the other remaining guests, had fallen back a little from Kearney and his bride in order to give Frank the necessary privacy and unimpeded opportunity of reading the pencilled scrawl.

They saw his face darken with annoyance. Rona, watching him closely, wondered what it could be. *If only it were something that would take Frank away for a few days, even tonight,* she thought, *but that would be asking too much of fate!*

Kearney chewed savagely on the cigar which he had thrust back between his teeth.

'You know what this says, Jim?' he barked. 'That goddam fool of a deputy sheriff—' He broke off, spluttering with anger, almost too furious to say more for the moment.

'What is it, Frank?' Rona's voice was low and calm and smooth, like a soft wind stirring the grasses and trees along the river. It was gentle now, but underneath ran the same latent strength that can turn a gentle summer breeze into a wild, surging storm.

It was the way Rona spoke, not the words she used, which calmed Frank down more than anything anyone else could have said. He threw the note on to the table.

'Seems like the sheriff's caught a man he figgers is Jesse Evans, Billy the Kid's saddle-

114

pard, an' they want me to identify him right away.'

'*Now?*' Rona's voice was softly incredulous. She successfully contrived to keep out any hint of the eagerness and wild hope which made her heart race under the tight corsage of her gown.

Disgust had replaced Frank's first surge of anger. There was even the faintest glow of satisfaction in him now as he realized more fully that only *he*, of all the people in the county, including the law officers themselves, only *he* could put his finger on this accomplice of William Bonney's and say with certainty, 'That is Jesse Evans.' He had a man's life in his hands, and the feeling of utter power that it gave him almost compensated for the damnable inconvenience of the time these people had chosen to call him in.

Of course, they had not *chosen* the time. Circumstances had just worked out that way and the climax of this situation was approaching, irrespective of his marriage or of anything else. These things were something quite outside the pattern which was evolving at the county seat. Kearney thought, with a peculiarly perverse humour, that it was a pity Jesse Evans, if it *were* him, had not chosen some more suitable time to be caught!

Both the county sheriff and this deputy Locke seemed all-fired scared that Bonney would somehow spring Evans from jail before they had time to convict him. They were rushing the case for tomorrow morning and Frank swore under his breath as he realized this would mean a tiresome and exhausting night ride with little, if any, sleep. But it was something that even Frank Kearney could not refuse to do, for, although the note had been politely, respectfully couched, there was no mistaking the fact that Locke did not expect any unnecessary shilly-shallying!

Inwardly Frank shuddered at what men would whisper behind his back if he attempted to put off this chore on account of it was his wedding night! That thought alone was sufficient to galvanize the Hackamore owner into action once he had had time to figure it all out.

'I'll have to go, my dear,' he said to his wife. 'I'm the only man in the whole county who can identify this Evans hombre, and it's my bounden duty to decide for the sheriff whether they've got the right man or not!'

Rona nodded, trying to appear merely as an understanding wife, suffering perhaps because in this man's world it was usually a woman's place to weep. But inwardly her heart was singing, though she knew it was but putting off the evil day. She was careful to mask her eyes, making them opaque, but the reaction of strain caused them to glisten moistly wet, so that Kearney felt good that his wife should be so disappointed, not because he was sadistic, but because it justified himself completely in his own eyes.

'Well, folks, I guess the party's over now. You-all heard I gotta do some riding, and I'm sure enough not forking a horse in *these* clothes. Help yourselves to a last drink while I go and change...'

He was back within ten minutes, no longer the bridegroom but the man of action, the Nemesis of all rustlers and wrongdoers.

He wore dark whipcord trousers tucked into spurred boots, a woollen shirt and scarf and an old corduroy jacket. Around his waist he had buckled a cartridge belt and a .38 Smith and Wesson protruded slightly from the holster on his right side.

Jim Grady was feeling a relief that almost matched Rona's, though the respective causes were hardly comparable.

Within twenty minutes from Jim Grady's first appearance at the house, Rona Kearney was watching the two men climb into leather in the moonlit yard.

She returned their salutes, watching as the riders clattered from the yard and headed out towards town. She was vaguely aware of the remaining guests departing and calling *'adios'* as wheels crunched and hooves pounded the gravel of the yard.

She stood for a long time in the shadow of

the roofed gallery, thinking, wondering if indeed Frank would get back by tomorrow night or whether fate might step in again and rescue her from something in which she had freely and willingly involved herself, but nevertheless did not want to materialize.

Not for the first time did she consider and seriously question the wisdom of her own actions.

Steve Jefford, her brother and her twin, had been struck down by Frank Kearney's hand and had died when riding with Bonney on one of his first lawless missions. Something inside Rona Jefford had died from that moment. Moreover, she did not have to be told of Steve's death; *she had known from the moment his life's blood had drained out!* And the rough men who had brought the news were thankful that this young girl had taken it all so calmly.

But from then on, Rona Jefford had thought only of avenging the other half of her – Steve – and had laid her plans accordingly. And the first step in the execution of these plans had taken nearly two years to complete. She was Kearney's wife now, married to the man who, in her eyes, had murdered her brother. The second part of her plan would be terminated and her revenge complete only when Frank Kearney was a broken man. Exactly how this would be accomplished Rona did not know. She had not planned the details, but she *did* know that she had the ability and the strength of purpose to see it through somehow, so that Steve's reproachful eyes would no longer haunt her to distraction...

CHAPTER VIII

'It's Tailor Made'

Although Red Twitchell normally retained a room at Trail House, it suited his purpose admirably on certain occasions to book one at Walker's Rooming House in the tougher quarter of the town.

Almost invariably he did this when a meeting was necessary, and Walker's Rooming House was an ideal place for any such secret conclave.

Tonight was no exception, and Red was seated at a table strewn with glasses and several bottles of liquor. The air was thick, as both door and windows were shut and *cigarrito* and cigar smoke hung heavily on the still, thick air.

Besides Red himself, there was the bearded Jack Cotter and six other men, all dressed in worn and soiled range-rig. Most of them were bearded, moustached or just plain unshaven. They were an evil-looking collection, each one wanted, in some place or another, for crimes ranging from crooked dealing to rustling and murder. Their crimes, however, sat lightly enough on them and evidently they were rarely, if ever, troubled by such stupid emotions as 'conscience' or 'finer feelings.'

Red Twitchell regarded them smilingly as he rolled and lit a smoke. He turned to Cotter, a big, well-muscled man with auburn hair and a short golden beard.

'Well, Jack,' Red drawled. 'You been ridin' some more since we saw a certain gent tonight. Let's have your report.'

Cotter hooked thumbs into his gun-belt and leaned back in his chair. 'You know where I went, Red,' he growled, 'and there ain't a lot to add.' Oddly, he was thinking as much about Ace Charro now as the riding he had done to-night. 'Bloody shame Ace couldn't 've let Kearney have it afore thet young skunk Escort shot him daid. Might've made our task easier with Frank outa the way–'

'I'll give you some news on Kearney presently,' Twitchell said. 'Now let's have *your* story for the benefit of the boys.'

'Wal, even was half of Hackamore in town today like a heerd, they sure been cuttin' out them critters plenty fast. I been all around that dog-leg section, Red, and, like I told you earlier, I figger they already got over five hun'ed head bedded down. They ain't stoppin' to do any brandin' as I could see; they's workin' like niggers to bring the stuff in.'

'Looks like the gather'll be ready much sooner than Ace figgered,' Twitchell drawled, looking at the others.

Cotter nodded. 'I'd say we could haze that stuff in a day or so. Should be a thousand haid at least by then. How does that sound?'

'It suits us all right,' Red said, 'except we'll haveta take care of the other matter more quickly now.' He left it at that, and Jack Cotter, knowing that the other men present were only to be concerned with the rustling of Kearney's stock, refrained from enlarging on what Twitchell referred to as 'the other matter.'

'How many men ridin' herd on thet bunch, Jack?' Red said.

'Four during daylight an' four at night. Once the herd's bedded down, they only figger to ride round 'em every so often. It looks like they's a coupla night-hawks on guard together while the other two sleeps. They gotta line cabin there—'

'Shouldn't be very difficult to settle with them – quietly,' Twitchell suggested, 'and drive off the herd without fuss?'

Jack Cotter nodded his big head emphatically. 'Easy as skinnin' a rabbit, Red,

121

just so long as we've got a half-dozen of our present company along.' He indicated the hard-eyed listening men ranged round the big table.

Cass Dickerson, who seemed to be the elected spokesman of the hard-case group, spoke up. 'When we settled with thesyer night-hawks, where we haze the stuff?'

Red said, 'It'll be south of the border where we'll have buyers waiting and ready with the *dinero*. But don't worry about those details. Jack an' me'll both be along–'

'How about thet Escort place?' Johnny Rideout, another of the owlhooters, asked. 'Won't they see or hear a herd thet size bein' hazed past their front gate an' start in wonderin'?'

'They would if they were there,' Twitchell smiled. 'Fact is they won't be there at-all. I heerd talk that the 'Paches are figgerin' to pay them back at last fer the lickin' Paul Escort gave 'em way back.'

There was a heavy, drawn-out silence whilst each man mulled over the significance of this casual remark in his mind.

'Kinda convenient, wouldn't it be, Red, them Injuns comin' down an' raidin' the place jest when we don't want no witnesses?' It was Cass Dickerson who asked the question, and Twitchell regarded him fixedly for a moment or two.

'I'd say it would be *very* convenient, Cass,'

he replied. His lips were smiling, but his green eyes were as cold as ice chips. Dickerson saw the danger of further questions and merely nodded.

'All right, Red,' he answered. 'We ain't here to ask questions as don't concern us. Jest so long as we know what we's goin' to do an' when we's goin' to get paid–'

'You'll get half the *dinero* day after tomorrow,' Twitchell told them, 'the rest you get when the beef's been safely delivered an' we return here at a time that I'll give you all later on. Right?'

Nods and grunts accepted this arrangement. No one was likely to do a fade-out at this stage, least of all Red Twitchell.

'What was it you was goin' to say about Kearney?' Cotter asked, sloshing liquor into his glass and rolling a quirly.

Red grinned. 'It shore seems like the devil looks after his own. I only jest heerd Kearney's gotta go to the county seat tonight an' identify some hombre the sheriff's locked up. Don't know how long he'll be away, but it may be time enough for us to clean up the whole thing–'

Cotter's eyes widened. 'You mean Kearney's ridin' *tonight,* Red, on his weddin' night an' leavin' thet yellow-haired filly–?'

'You keep yore mind on the chore ahead, Jack,' Twitchell replied coldly. 'That's one way you could meet grief and a leaden pill;

the other, you'll have gold in your pockets enough to buy a dozen women as good as her–'

'Or as bad,' Cass Dickerson laughed coarsely...

After Cass, Johnny and the rest of them had quit the room, Twitchell turned to Cotter.

'There's something else, Jack, which has fallen into our laps since you took that second ride tonight.'

'Something good?' Cotter grinned.

'It's tailor-made,' Red agreed. 'You remember Charlie an' me discussin' the possibility of Kearney offering Escort a job?'

Cotter nodded. 'Don't say it's come off?'

'It sure has. I been keepin' eyes an' ears open while you was checkin' on the herd guards, an' it's a cert now that Escort's ridin' for Hackamore. He came back to town with his sister around nine o'clock, on his way back to the horse-ranch. That was when I saw a county deputy come ridin' hell for leather into town. I found out *his* visit is tied in with Kearney havin' to go to the county seat. Jim Grady of Hackamore rode out to bring Kearney in–'

'An' you heerd about thet bustard Escort?'

'It's common gossip by now that Escort's ridin' for Hackamore as from dawn tomorrow. That means–'

'It means,' Cotter grinned evilly, 'that any time after tomorrow mornin' we kin get to

124

work on the Escort place, doesn't it?'

Twitchell nodded. 'There's just one thing I want you to do, Jack. It concerns Sarah Escort–'

'Sary? That's his kid sister?'

'Yes, and I want her right here in town when we're giving it to the old folks!'

'Ain't thet liable to be risky, leavin' her out of it as well as Paul, an' how you goin' to fix for her to be in Lariat?'

Twitchell laughed. 'Sarah Escort's too purty a filly to be violated and killed by *Apaches*. You'll ride out early an' make sure that Paul's already left for Hackamore. Then you'll deliver Sarah an urgent message from *me* concerning her brother. It'll be urgent enough for the Escorts to let you bring her back to town–'

'What you goin' to do with her then?' Cotter grinned.

'Dump her in Trail House for the time bein'. Then we'll be on our way. After that she'll *haveta* remain in town and *I'll* be her protector!'

'What kinda story will you tell Paul when he finds out? It'll haveta be a good one!'

'It'll be good all right,' Twitchell smiled, 'and if he doesn't swallow it along with the Injun story, then–' Red paused and patted the holstered gun at his side.

'But thet hombre's faster than anything I ever saw, Red. Sure, you're handy with a

125

flame-thrower, but mebbe you ain't seen Paul Escort in action like I have!'

'Who said anything about a gunfight?' Twitchell asked. 'Even if he's the fastest gunfighter in the whole west, he cain't very well beat a bullet in the back!'

Cotter laughed and finished his drink. 'I guess you got everythin' worked out, Red,' he guffawed as he picked up his hat and stepped from the room...

Jed Segal came out of the bunkhouse walking leisurely towards the big corral at Hackamore. He saw the rider swing through the open gates of the yard and felt a mild pleasure that this Escort fellow had arrived early in spite of his late riding last night. It mean, in all probability, that he was a willing worker, even though he would likely need showing a good few wrinkles.

'Howdy, Escort,' the ramrod greeted. 'Frank told me you was to report for work first thing this mornin'. You ever choused cattle before?'

Paul returned Segal's greeting and slid from leather. 'I'm no top-hand, Jed,' he grinned, 'but I'm ready to learn the way Hackamore does things.'

Segal nodded and rolled a smoke, leaning against the poles of the corral. 'You'll need a pony and a rope, but your saddle looks okay–'

'I'd sooner ride the gelding, if it's all the same,' Paul said, trailing the reins over the animal's head. 'I've ridden this one at round-ups and he knows cattle.'

Segal observed that the big gelding remained 'ground-anchored' without attempting to move his feet. That bore out the truth of Escort's claim.

'They's no reason why you shouldn't ride your own saddler if he's a good cow-hoss,' Segal agreed. 'You'll still want a rope. How's about that rifle? Is it the Winchester that Charro tried to use on Frank?'

Paul nodded. 'Toomis seemed to figure I had a right to it. Spoils of war!'

Segal grinned. 'Why, I guess that's right, Paul. Soon as I've caught an' saddled my hoss you'd best come on over an' meet the boys. They's a good bunch but they's a few thick heads this mornin'. They're finding it hard slogging to get started.'

Paul watched while Segal paid out his rope and adjusted the noose. Everything about the man was casual as he worked and quietly opened the gate into the corral. Evidently he had already selected the pony he would ride, for the rope snaked out suddenly and without warning, catching a piebald in mid-stride, the noose settling gently but restrainingly over the animal's head and neck.

There was no wild tugging at the rope and Segal was able to bring the pony in easily without exerting any pull on his lariat.

In a matter of seconds the animal was saddled and bridled. Jed made a last adjustment to the cinch-buckle and slowly straightened up. He picked up a ready-coiled lariat from a fence post and handed it to Paul, who hung it over his saddle-horn.

Segal was about to lead the new rider towards the bunkhouse when both men became aware that a woman was standing on the gallery of the house.

She came down the steps slowly, shading her eyes against the brightness of the lifting sun. She called out in a low yet reaching voice, 'Jed! If that's Escort, send him over for a moment, will you?'

'The boss's wife's up right early for her first day,' Segal said quietly. 'Mebbe she's kinda deputizing for Frank while he's away. You'd best go over an' see what she wants.'

Escort nodded, dropping the reins which he had picked up and moving with long, easy strides towards the house. He removed his sun-faded hat and stood looking down at the woman who was now mistress of Frank Kearney's home.

He said, 'Good morning, ma'am,' and waited for her to speak.

She regarded him in silence for a moment, her rain-grey eyes moving over his face almost as though she were *searching* for something.

She smiled then, and it was a smile of warmth, reaching her eyes and curving her red lips pleasantly. The sombre beauty of her changed, in that moment, to something more sparkling and animated.

'I haven't had much chance to talk to you, Mr Escort, except for the few words we managed to have together yesterday evening. I know Frank has taken you on here and I know about the cheque for your folks, but I wanted to thank you again myself; to make you understand how much I – we appreciate the fact that you probably jeopardized your life to save that of a man you didn't know and probably had never seen. You didn't know Frank, did you?'

He was surprised at the question and shook his head, smiling a little.

What difference would it have made, he wondered, if I *had* known Frank Kearney?

'No, ma'am, I never met Frank – Mr Kearney – until yesterday, as far as I know.' He paused and then added rather hurriedly, 'It was just a chore to earn a few dollars and help out Toomis. I figure Toomis as a right kind of hombre–'

She saw that he was only uncomfortable when it came to expressing some inner feelings or when he was called upon to talk about himself. These were qualities almost unique amongst the men she had met. Even the lovable Steve had been a mite brash and boastful and had never hesitated to recount his deeds with almost childlike enthusiasm.

'You – you must be terribly fast with a gun, Escort, but you don't look like a – gunfighter!'

'I'm not,' Paul said, 'and I'm not sure *I* know what a gunfighter looks like anyway!'

'Billy the Kid–' she began and then bit her lip and closed her mouth over whatever it was she would have said.

'Already folks are calling you the Gentle Gunman,' she said, turning her gaze now towards the corrals, where the men were saddling up their mounts.

'I have heard that, ma'am,' Escort said, 'but I don't seek out men and I don't relish killing. Sometimes I guess it's necessary, as like yesterday, for instance–'

She nodded. 'I think I understand. Frank said that you were to arrange with Jed whenever you want to visit your folks. He told me last night before – well, he was called away suddenly on – business.' The pale, almost olive skin became slightly suffused with pink.

Paul nodded. 'I know. I was in town when the county deputy rode in on a half-dead horse. I was in the marshal's office, so I know they wanted Frank up at the county seat to identify this man Jesse Evans.'

She said, 'Mr Kearney – Frank – expects to be home tonight, but he said for me to tell you about taking time off, just in case he was delayed getting back.'

'I guess that's mighty civil of him, Mrs Kearney, ma'am,' Paul said. 'There's something I want to fix over to home pretty soon. We were figgering on getting a boy to help out now that I won't be there.'

'You see Jed when you want to ride over,' Rona Kearney smiled. 'He'll fix something for you.'

She was gone in a sudden whirl of skirts, leaving him with the memory of that *questing* expression in her eyes, before the smile had livened her face and chased away the sober set to her features. He was left with something else, even more tangible. The perfume of her hair still clung to his nostrils as he turned on his heel and walked towards Segal and the Hackamore crew...

It was noon of the second day. All morning eight riders, including Jed Segal and Paul Escort, had been chousing mossyhorns and mavericks from the brush and brakes along the Chico's bottomlands south-east of the town.

Paul experienced no hardship in long hours in the saddle, and his strength was such that, if necessary, he could bulldoze a steer with astonishing ease.

However, bulldozing was normally reserved for rodeos or for some dire emergency, as when a steer turned on a rider who had been thrown from his horse. Otherwise the trick was to whirl a loop over horns and head or else for the more expert rope artists to throw low and catch a fore-leg, sending the beast crashing to the ground with a minimum of trouble. Paul was no adept at this more spectacular method, but, having roped horses almost from the time he had been born, he found it not much more difficult to rope a long-horned brush-popper or a skittish maverick.

Now the sweating cowboys were hunkered down for the noon meal, whilst they kept a wary eye on the stuff they had so far rounded up. Later, this gather, along with others, would be hazed down to holding grounds, prior to cutting out the stuff required for the trail drive.

Segal said, munching jerky and biscuits, 'Frank figgered to be back late last night. He hadn't shown up by first thing this morning.'

'Mebbe he's havin' himself a good time while he's up there,' Slim Massey, a tall Texan, suggested.

'What! an' him only jest married?' Crick Rowland snorted. 'Would *you* stay on in a big town, Slim, was you married to Rona Kearney?'

For all that these men were a good bunch, easy-going and hard-working, they were not above a coarse joke, and somehow Paul Escort felt he didn't want to hear any obvious or even veiled suggestions in connection with Rona and Frank Kearney.

'There's something I want to get fixed at home, Jed,' he said quickly, switching the conversation.

'There's a kid in town I know who might be ready to use a job at my father's place. I'd like to see him first and then ride on and tell my folks, if I could have the time? I'll do a spell of night-riding tonight, if you like, and make up for it.'

Segal swallowed the last of his grub and reached for his canteen, swallowing noisily before making reply. He wiped his mouth on his hand and regarded Escort with a friendly eye.

'You take off right away, Paul. You ain't made out too bad for a tenderfoot this last day and a half. As to night-ridin', we'll see. I guess you'll get your bellyful of it.'

Paul thanked the ramrod, and such was Segal's quiet authority and Escort's eagerness for hard work that no one of the six riders there resented Paul's request or envied him his quiet ride to town and thence on to his folks' home...

CHAPTER IX

Tragedy

Escort rode the familiar trail south of the Rio Chico with a variety of feelings, mixed and conflicting, within his breast.

He ought to be as happy as any man could be, so the simple and direct side of his nature proclaimed.

He had fixed, albeit temporarily, with young George Welcome to start work at William Escort's ranch once he had arranged things with his father and mother. Welcome was no more than coming up seventeen, but Paul knew that he did not care overmuch for the work he did in Lariat, helping Colton, the town blacksmith. George, who also loved horses, had jumped at the tentative offer Paul had made. Moreover, in young Welcome's eyes, Paul Escort was a knight in shining armour; a slayer of dragons; a man who could deal effectively with the Ace Charros and the Jack Cotters of this wild frontier.

Thus Paul had put his proposition and, provided William and Martha were agreeable, George would undoubtedly make a good and happy worker and his services would rate less than half of what they would have to pay a man.

Paul himself was happy in his job, yet the close proximity of Rona Kearney worried him. It was a shadow on his sunlit world, yet not a dark black shadow to fear, but lightly shaded and wonderfully coloured, and yet still a shadow.

He told himself that, once Frank had returned, he would scarcely, if ever, see Mrs Kearney. Strange how her name sounded when given the protecting legal prefix of 'Mrs'.

He felt his cheeks darken again as he realized that too often he thought of her as Rona Kearney, or worse – as Rona. She was young, he considered, not above twenty or twenty-one years, and the incongruity of regarding her as youthful when she was as old, or perhaps a little older, than himself did not occur to him.

He pulled the gelding to a walk, not because it showed sign of undue distress, but because the afternoon sun was pouring down a stronger heat today. The slower gait of the horse allowed Paul to think and to re-examine the vague and nebulous dreams that he had always held but had never dared to explore fully.

He tired to figure out how much he could save out of his pay each month after buying necessities and allowing his parents, or at least Sarah, some small amount. And then he laughed out loud as he speculated on how many cowboys – even top-hands – ever saved sufficient from their pay to start their own brand. Precious few, he reckoned, and grinned, and then the grin faded and Paul Escort's face became a frozen mask of horror...

He had come within sight of the ranch now, close enough in to see that it was a ranch no longer, but a smoke-blackened and partial ruin. His strong hands tightened unconsciously on the reins so that the gelding's head was drawn back hard. He only realized this when the animal began to rear. His grip slackened a little as he put the horse to a gallop, giving it the pressure of his knees as it sailed over the pole fence which circumnavigated the yard. He pulled up in a cloud of swirling dust no more than ten paces from the dark, open doorway and, without being aware of what he was doing, slid from leather and trailed the gelding's reins.

Shock held him rigid, then, for the space of seconds on end. His nostrils became filled with the stench of kerosene and charred wood; the stink of death was a foul stain on the air.

The 'dobe ranch-house itself still stood, merely smoke-blackened and apparently intact, but doors and windows, the barns at the side, everything that would burn, was little more than a pile of ashes and smouldering remains.

He stepped round to the side of the house and put his gaze to the meadows and the nearer corrals, but there was no sign of a gelding that Paul could see.

Steeling himself to the task ahead, he returned to the doorway of the house. The door itself was no more than a crumbling mass of charred pieces. There was enough sunlight pouring into the house from empty door and window for Paul to be able to glimpse something of the fiendish wreck and destruction inside.

He stepped across the threshold, all feeling in him still paralysed from the hideous shock of this Apache-inspired atrocity. A vague thought flitted at the back of his mind that it was strange the Apaches should have struck so fast, the one time he had been away from home for a night. But the thought became lost in the turmoil of his dazed brain.

The same devilishly thorough hands had been at work inside the house; nothing that would burn had escaped the flames; the air in here reeked even more strongly of kerosene and death.

He found them after a time, half buried beneath beams which had fallen from the low ceiling. There was scarcely anything left;

nothing recognizable; nothing to identify them except a few bone buttons and scraps of hard leather from boots, a belt buckle; such things. Dimly to Paul's staggered brain came the realization that there were only *two* things which had once been human. He searched frantically now, passing from wrecked living room to gutted bedroom. He worked and moved with a feverish, desperate haste, trying not to give himself time to think but lifting aside every piece of timber, every burned frame of furniture in the fearful dread of discovering the third body.

At last he went outside and filled his lungs with air which, by comparison, tasted sweet and clean; something God-given and pure in a man-made world of fearful things. Eventually he moved towards the gelding with the slow, measured steps of a sleep-walker. He lifted down the canteen from the horn and drank the lukewarm, life-giving water, restoppering the flask and returning it. If there had been a pint bottle of whisky in his *alforja* pouch, Paul would have drunk the lot, there and then. For the first time in his life he needed something outside of himself to lend him strength.

But, strangely, the water he had swallowed seemed to help. It had relieved the abominable dryness in his mouth, the thickness of his tongue and the parched, arid feeling in his throat. He moistened his lips, touched the gun at his hip almost instinctively, and set about the task of making a detailed search of the gutted outbuildings.

He must have spent two hours at least, judging by the sun, before he walked slowly back to the yard, one searing thought uppermost in his mind. He was certain now that Sarah, at least, had been spared the terrible fate of his parents, and then, riding on the heels of that thought, another idea rocked him as he stood with trembling hands fashioning a *cigarrito. Suppose the Indians had carried Sarah off? What other explanation could there be for the fact that her body was not here?*

Gradually he became aware of physical things, such as a renewed thirst, pain in his hands and fingers and dull aches in his muscles. Even then he scarcely realized the Herculean task he had accomplished in single-handedly moving every huge, charred cross-beam, every piece of débris, both large and small, whole doors on the barns which had only partially burned before crashing to the floor.

He looked down at his dirty and bloody hands, full of splinters and black with charcoal. His shirt was filthy and torn and sweat runnelled the blackness on his face into paler streaks.

He stumbled around to where the lean-to 'dobe stable still stood minus doors and roof. He found a smoke-blackened bucket and thrust it under the pump, working the handle and sloshing the cool water until the bucket was full.

He sluiced his face, hands and arms, unmindful of the water as it streamed down and soaked his shirt. He stood in the sun, letting its warmth dry him and imbue into him some of its cosmic life-strength.

He built another smoke from the sack and papers he had left in his coat pocket. His mind was still a dull ache but his thoughts were becoming gradually clearer. He even found that his limbs were responding more readily and that his hands, now clean, shook appreciably less.

Time rolled on and the sun lowered itself towards the tips of the Smoke Signals. Then it was that Escort heard the sound of hoof-beats on the trail. He clawed for his gun and it was out, naked and shining in the sun's slanting rays, a machine of death, death for as many as six men if he were careful enough. Then he remembered the ten-shot carbine and stepped forward to pluck it from the saddle scabbard, only to stop with his hand on the stock as he recognized Marshal Rich Toomis down the trail a way...

He let the carbine fall back into place and slowly, mechanically dropped the six-gun into its holster.

Toomis' seamed face was set in bleak,

harsh lines as he rode slowly into the yard, his gaze traversing the terrible scene before pinning itself to the rigid figure of Escort.

He stepped from leather and ground-anchored his horse, careful as he moved forward to avoid the faint tracks which his experienced eye had noticed.

He waited for Escort to speak, and for a while Paul just stood and stared at him; *through* him as though seeing something far off. Paul, remembering the *cigarrito,* took down a final puff of smoke before grinding the stub under his boot-heel. He looked up then and into the marshal's pitying eyes.

'My parents,' he said jerkily, forcing the words out with an effort. 'Both of them, but there's no trace of Sarah–'

'We'll get whoever's responsible fer this, Escort, if we have to comb the Smoke Signals single-handed. But we won't do that; I'll get every goddamed county sheriff and deputy down and every able-bodied man for a posse, soon as we know which way we gotta trail out.'

'Help me bury them, Marshal. That's all we can do for them now. Afterwards we've *got* to find Sarah – somehow–'

Toomis nodded and began issuing his orders, purely to galvanize Paul into activity and relieve the strain on his mind. 'I'll get spades and we'll start digging, Paul. I guess mebbe they'd like to rest over in the

meadows yonder, in the shadow of the bluff.'
He walked towards the house, going carefully and peering for the sign he expected to find, however lightly made – that of moccasined feet and unshod hoofs.

He made his complete circle of the house and was gone nearly a half-hour.

He had found a couple of saddle blankets, scorched only, and carefully he wrapped the charred remnants in each, toting the grisly burdens singly and with considerable effort to the place where Paul was digging.

They worked on in the gathering twilight, fashioning one grave which would hold both blanket-covered forms. After a while, Toomis loped back to the gutted barns and, miraculously, found a storm lantern which had not burned or exploded its contents.

By the flickering yellow light they lowered the bodies in, and huskily, but with a deep sincerity, Marshal Rich Toomis said the Lord's Prayer and the Twenty-Third Psalm – the only two biblical passages he knew.

Paul, with eyes moist, knew that some day he would thank the grizzled old Indian fighter for this help he was giving, and the spiritual support and sympathy was as important as the physical. But right now he didn't want to talk about it. Instead, he set his mind on the thought of retribution, only dimly wondering how one man, or even a sheriff's posse, could ever track down the perpetrators of this vile crime.

The grave was covered now and they stood for a moment bare-headed in the lantern and starlight. Soon, the moon would be rising, but now these two silent men were nebulous shapes with a dark mound of freshly turned sods between them.

Shortly, Toomis picked up the spades and handed the lantern to Paul, silently leading the way back to the ranch-yard where the horses still stood with trailing reins.

Toomis found some undamaged grain in a bin and, after feeding both horses, he watered them at the trough behind the house. He returned, leading them with the reins looped over his arm and hauled up close to the wooden figure of Escort.

Toomis reached into his saddle pocket and withdrew a pint bottle. Tentatively, half afraid, he offered it, and Paul put the bottle to his lips and drank deeply before returning it wordlessly.

The velvety, star-spangled sky whirled around and the fence and yard performed incredible feats in front of his screwed-up eyes. Then the landscape righted itself and he felt the warm spirit hit his belly and the fumes begin to deaden some of the pain inside him.

Toomis took a swig and replaced the nearly empty bottle before rolling a couple of smokes and passing one across to Paul.

The match flared in his cupped hands and, as though that were a signal, the rising moon began to show through the cottonwoods.

Toomis said, 'What are you going to do, Paul? Right now, I mean?'

'Ride back to Hackamore, I guess. What else? I've got me a job there, as you know. Later, mebbe, they'll give me time off to take the trail to the mountains, else I'll just have to quit.'

'I cut sign when I was looking around earlier on,' the marshal said, trying to choose his words carefully. 'I was looking for moccasin prints and tracks of unshod ponies. Instead I found two sets of boot tracks and some sign of *shod* horses–'

'Mine,' Paul said woodenly.

Toomis shook his head. 'I saw *your* tracks, all right, where you stepped down from your gelding. There were two *other* sets, Paul, and the horseshoe prints was different–'

'What are you trying to tell me, Rich?' Escort's voice was a low croak of anguish.

'This wasn't no 'Pache raid, Paul. Sure, it was made to look like one, *but this deviltry was done by white men!*'

It was so long before Escort replied that Toomis wondered whether or not the significance of his disclosure had penetrated Escort's mind. It must have been a full minute before he spoke. 'I don't believe any white man could be so debased and vile, Rich. And who could benefit by such a dastardly act? Money? There was practically none in the house, and if there had been, why should robbers murder and burn–'

'I guess I don't know the answers – yet, son,' Toomis growled, 'but, Bigawd, I'll make it my business to find out, surely.'

Paul had been thinking, remembering now that the marshal was an old Indian campaigner. He remembered once hearing in town that Toomis was wellnigh as good at cutting sign as an Apache or a Mex. And this marshal of an obscure frontier town was no braggart, nor a man to sit back and let others do the work. *Toomis knew what he was talking about!* The realization came suddenly to Escort, and it was as though there were no room left in him for further shock. He had reached his full capacity; even if he found that Sarah had been killed or taken prisoner to be turned into a slave – even that knowledge, he felt, could add little more to his silent and indrawn grief. Again this long silence before he spoke.

'You saw nothing when you were riding here, Rich?'

'Nary a thing,' Toomis said. 'I took time off to ride around as I do once in a way. I'd been circling around Hackamore's trail gather over to the dog-leg section. That's how come I was near here. Afterwards I jest moseyed down to pay my respects to your folks. Then I saw–'

Paul said, 'I guess you're right. About this not bein' Indian work, I mean. There's no uprising–'

'I'd wager there ain't a redman within two-three hundred miles of here, Paul, nor has been for months now.'

Escort nodded. 'I guess we better be hitting the trail, Rich. I'm riding back to town with you and make some enquiries about Sarah. There's just a chance someone might have heard something or seen her riding perhaps–'

'Wait a minute,' Toomis said, gripping Paul's arm. 'We don't know yet fer certain that harm's come to her. Mebbe she rode into town on an errand. Ah, Paul, I wouldn't go building too strong on my hunches, but I gotta feeling Sarah's mebbe all right!'

Paul wrung the lawman's hand in the moon- and star-spangled night and then turned and slowly stepped into saddle.

It was a long time before the silence was broken, and then it was Escort who spoke, when the lights of Lariat appeared like twinkling stars low down across the tree- and brush-fringed Chico.

'They'll be giving me another name soon, Rich,' he said in a low voice. 'Somehow I don't figure the Gentle Gunman will sound quite right.'

But Paul Escort was wrong. His soubriquet was not destined to be changed. Yet, had he been able to face the murderers of his parents at this moment, there would have been no gentleness in his heart or in that right hand of his, holding the gun...

So they came into Lariat at around nine o'clock, and when Paul heard his name called from the doorway of Trail House he stiffened in the saddle, scarcely daring to turn and look. *For the voice that spoke his name was the voice of Sarah Escort!*

He felt the marshal's hand reach out and grip his arm, and Toomis's words penetrated into his fogged mind.

'Take et easy, Paul. It's Sarah all right, an' she's safe and sound over to Trail House.'

Paul turned his head slowly, seeing the familiar face and figure of his sister limned in the hotel lights, and he knew he was not dreaming. He lifted his hand in acknowledgment, and Sarah waved gaily.

Toomis said: 'You don't want an audience when you tell her the news, son. Go on over to the office and wait there while I fetch her over!'

Escort nodded and reined the gelding to the other side of the street, while the marshal drew up alongside the walk fronting the hotel...

147

CHAPTER X

In a Small, Dusty Room

Inside the marshal's office, Sarah stared in perplexity at the harsh set of her brother's face. Toomis, also, was of such sober countenance that she knew immediately that something was radically wrong.

'I'll fix some coffee for us, if I kin get this danged stove to burn up,' Rich Toomis grunted, busying himself with the damper and applying fresh fuel to the stove.

And, whilst he banged about with coffee pot and cups, Paul broke the news as gently as possible to Sarah.

He saw her face pale, and for a moment she fought to retain her upright position in the chair. Horror showed its ugly image in her wide eyes. Twice she opened her mouth to speak and twice no words came.

Toomis came forward and silently handed each of them a cup of steaming java which he had covertly laced with whisky.

When they hesitated he growled, 'Drink it up the both of you; it'll shore do you a heap of good.'

They obeyed, sipping the scalding liquid

and feeling some of its strength seep into their bones.

'But for the grace of God, Sarah, you would– How is it you're in town?'

'It was Mr Twitchell who came and asked – Ma and Pa if they would let me go to town with Red. He has a sister in Albuquerque and wants to send her a real swell dress for her birthday present.

'Of course,' Sarah continued in a dull, flat voice, 'Red knows girls in town, but none around my measurements–'

'What are you talking about, Sis?' Paul demanded. He hadn't called her that since many years; an indication that he was now both father and mother to Sarah, as well as big brother.

'I'm tryin' to tell you, Paul. Red's sister is about the same height and build as myself. Red figured if Hattie Truelove, the dress-maker, could use me as a model, he'd surely have a dress that would really fit his sister–'

'When did he ride over an' ask you?' Toomis said.

'Why, I guess it was soon after Paul had lit out for Hackamore, day before yesterday. Why do you ask?'

'No special reason,' Rich Toomis said, ''ceptin' we're almighty glad he did ask you here.' He gave Paul a fixed look and added: 'There's no doubt that they's a bunch o' red devils on the warpath, an' lucky for you and

Paul Twitchell got you back to Lariat before they struck. You'll haveta stay on here at Trail House fer a while, I guess, 'less Paul's got any other idees.'

Escort wondered about keeping the vital piece of information from Sarah – that the raid was made by white and not red men. In recounting the story he had kept to the bare facts, as briefly as possible, and had not yet mentioned that, through the marshal's sign-cutting, they both knew for certain that this devilry was not Indian inspired.

Toomis had a reason for not letting on about this, and Paul felt the least he could do was to respect Rich's wishes. The man had helped him, down there, at the scene of the slaughter, and Paul owed it to him to back up Toomis in this deceit. He could see now that Rich wanted everyone in town to believe that both the law *and* Paul and Sarah had unquestionably swallowed the idea that the murder of the elder Escorts and the burning of the ranch had been the work of savages.

Paul said presently, 'I'll have to be getting back to Hackamore soon, Rich. Mebbe when you get time you could ride down – down to the – ranch and see whether any of the geldings bolted to the foothills. If so, mebbe they'll be back, and we'll need to bring them to the livery.'

'I'll do that, Paul, an' keep an eye on Sary

as well–'

'Couldn't you stay with Abby Gates, or someone, Sarah?' Paul suggested. 'I'd somehow feel happier if you were with friends.'

'Why, I guess Abby wouldn't mind for a spell,' Sarah said. 'She's been inviting me for weeks. Now I can take her up on that offer!'

'You do, Sis,' Escort said. 'Now I'll see you back to Trail House and then light out for Hackamore.'

But Paul didn't return to Kearney's place at once. Instead, he crossed back to the marshal's office. There were several things he wanted to discuss now that Sarah had gone back.

He found the new night marshal had come in; he was not due to take over from Toomis until ten o'clock. This John Hooley, it seemed, had not been in Lariat long. But he had worn law badges in Taos, Socorro and Silver City. His reputation, both with a gun and in bringing in criminals, was as good as that of most United States marshals or Pinkerton operatives.

Paul took to this lean, raw-boned man with the Chinaman moustaches and the hard, grey eyes. It was not long before Hooley had the whole story of the recent happenings at the Escort ranch.

John Hooley didn't say much beyond asking a few pointed questions, and presently Toomis spoke again.

151

'Thanks for keeping quiet in front of Sarah, Paul, about the prints we found of white men. I didn't have time to warn you before, but I figger it's best if we let everyone think we're blaming the Indians for this!'

'You figger, mebbe, whoever did this might get careless if they think they've gotten away with it?'

'Sure. Don't you? For some reason *some* yellow-livered bustards wanted you Escorts out of the way. Why, I cain't yet figger out–'

'This story of the man Twitchell you told me,' John Hooley murmured. 'It sounds kinda *thin* to me. It's surely a strange coincidence that the exact time this Twitchell chooses to whisk Escort's sister up here to town is the moment – or just before – chosen by some skunk to kill and burn–'

'But Sarah explained all that, Hooley–' Toomis began.

But John Hooley shook his head. 'I'm still not satisfied. I'm an outsider, remember, an' don't know the people concerned in this. Never met Twitchell or Sarah Escort yet, as I mind, and only known Paul here a few moments. I reckon that gives me a kinda edge!

'Another thing. When you-all told this story, you said somethin' about Twitchell offerin' you a coupla thousand dollars for that ranch – much more, in your own words, than it was worth. What about that?'

Toomis and Escort exchanged glances, and in the eyes of each was the first, faint dawning of a horrible suspicion.

Toomis at length broke the long, drawn-out silence.

'Supposing,' he said, 'that what you got in yore mind, Hooley, is right. Tell me why any hombre would offer two thousand cash for a 'dobe house an' horse graze bought for a dollar an' a quarter an acre an' then *murder* an' *burn* when the offer is refused?'

'I guess I cain't figger all the angles, Toomis, right now. And then again, I savvy so little about the folks concerned.

'F'r instance. Was this Twitchell man putting up the money himself? And what work does he do–?'

'That's just it, Marshal,' Escort said. 'He *doesn't* work as far as anyone knows. He wears range-rig an' forks a three-hundred-dollar horse, but he sure doesn't ride for any spread in the whole valley.

'As to putting up the money, he claimed he was just an agent for a cattle and horse syndicate. They had plans *and* money, for development – so Twitchell told us.'

The night marshal tamped tobacco into a short briar, lit up and puffed clouds of blue smoke. He addressed himself to Rich Toomis.

'You know anything of any syndicate that

might be interested in a few acres of grama grass and a 'dobe house? I'm guessing that, for horses, the acreage wouldn't be vast.'

'No, it sure ain't vast. Enough good grass and a few alfalfa fields to maintain thirty-fifty geldings through summer and winter,' Toomis told him. 'I ain't ever heerd of any concern interested in this part of the country, though.'

'Rustling hereabouts?' Hooley asked, cocking an eyebrow.

'Nothing to speak of. A few critters run off now and again mebbe, but Hackamore runs so many head they wouldn't know 'less a sizeable herd was cut out.'

'Well,' John Hooley said, 'I got me some ideas on this, but as yet they're no more than guesses. I reckon I'll make it my business to meet Mr Twitchell right soon. Who else you figger we ought to keep our eyes on?'

'I'll point some of 'em out to you tonight. We kin make a tour of the deadfalls. It's after ten now, but I ain't got anythin' special to do.'

'And I must be getting back to Kearney–' Paul rose to his feet.

'It don't look like Frank's back yet,' Toomis grunted. 'Leastway's, he wasn't on the stage. I guess he's havin' to stay over longer'n he figgered.'

Paul shrugged. 'Makes but little differ-

154

ence. Jed Segal's a good enough range-boss, I'd say. The work'll go on whether Frank's there or not, meaning nothing against Kearney...'

'It went smooth as silk, Charlie.' Red Twitchell grinned, seating himself at the table in Widgeon's rear office.

'Escort and Toomis rode in a while back, an' already talk's circulatin' that the marshal's aimin' to raise a posse, when he decides which direction he's gotta take!'

'How come Escort's in town again?' Widgeon asked, pouring himself, and then Red, a drink.

'Cotter's been keepin' his ears open, an' it seems Escort was fixin' to hire the Welcome kid for his ranch. Fer sure, either Escort or Toomis, or both of 'em, have been down there today and seen the mess.'

'You didn't leave any witnesses, Red?'

'There weren't any to leave. The old folks got a bullet each before we fired the place. The girl Sarah was already in town.' Red didn't consider it necessary or desirable to go into that part of the story.

He had given some considerable thought to the question of enticing Sarah to town without arousing any suspicion, and his first idea – of sending Jack Cotter with a message – hadn't seemed very good, on second thoughts.

155

Then it was that he had hit on the idea of sending a present to his sister in Albuquerque, and evolved a plan asking Sarah to act as model for the dress which Hattie Truelove was already making. The cream of the jest, Red thought, lay in the fact that he really *did* have a sister in Albuquerque – a saloon girl like Corinne, only worse – and he had every intention of sending the dress once it was finished and paid for. Red Twitchell figured he had covered his tracks pretty well. Later, perhaps, that fool Escort could be dealt with, much as Red had suggested to Jack Cotter the other day.

'Then you're about set to move that bunch soon as it's a right size,' Charlie Widgeon said in his soft, oily voice. 'The sooner we get that *dinero,* the better I'll like it. So far it's been nothing but pay out–'

'Well, I've saved you a cool two thousand, Charlie, and Ace has saved you *his* cut by gettin' himself bumped.

'As to movin' the stuff, we're ready to start in right away. Like I said, the Hackamore riders haven't bin slouches over this roundup. The herd's waitin', bedded down with only four riders guarding it–'

'Tonight?' Widgeon whispered, and Red Twitchell nodded and grinned.

'Tonight's as good a night as any, Charlie, and Cotter's already warned the boys. Everything's falling into our laps – even

Kearney's still away–'

'What difference does that make, Red?' Widgeon said sharply. '*He* wouldn't be night-herding, 'specially with a new wife he hasn't even–'

'It's better this way,' Red interrupted. 'Kearney's got a mighty bad habit of showing up at the wrong time, like he did way back when they nabbed young Jesse Evans, and later, when he almost caught Charro red-handed.'

Widgeon nodded. 'Yes. I guess it is better to get this stuff down and across the border while Frank's still away. Just so long as you don't leave a broad trail–'

'There won't be any trail, the route we're takin', Charlie. Once they hit that shale stretch and then edge along the desert, there won't be enough sign even for a 'Pache to smell out. By morning the wind'll have erased any prints on the desert. What's more, it wouldn't surprise me none if we had a storm tonight. I seen clouds massing up over the Smoke Signals. I guess that would be dandy, except night ridin' in the pouring rain's a goddam awful chore.'

'It's the easiest and fastest way of earning five hundred dollars, Red.' Widgeon smiled. 'It'd take you a year as a forty a month ranny to collect that amount of *dinero, and* doing ten hours in the saddle very day...'

In a small, dusty and junk-littered room

above Charlie Widgeon's office, Corinne raised her head from the knot hole in the rough pine-wood floor, the underneath side of which, whitewashed over, did service as the ceiling in Charlie's office.

The girl's face was ashen, and the rouge stood out on her face and lips in grotesque, clown-like contrast to the whiteness beneath.

Her knees were shaking so much that she had difficulty in getting to her feet. Once she stumbled and nearly collided with a stack of broken chairs which shifted suddenly and threatened to fall to the floor with a crash. She felt as though her heart had stopped beating, but the chairs locked again before they had slipped too far, and slowly, fearfully, Corrine tip-toed from this room from where she had eavesdropped on the most hideous, nightmare conversation she had ever heard.

In the privacy of her small room, with a few minutes to spare before she need make an appearance in the saloon, she thought about the things Red had told Charlie, whilst she tried desperately to control the shaking of her limbs and the pounding of her heart under the low corsage of her yellow dress.

Corinne Devereux had never been an entirely virtuous woman. Such a thing was scarcely possible for one of her trade on the untamed frontier. But like so many of her easy-going kind, she had, underneath the hard exterior, not only a soft heart, but even some fiercely clung-to principles. She was used enough to saloon brawls, and even the occasional killings which resulted and were more often done in self defence. Paul Escort, in Corinne's mind, as well as in the Law's, would have been perfectly justified in killing Jack Cotter when the latter had drawn first. And Paul had *had* to shoot Charro in order to save Kearney's life. Such things were clear and understandable to Corinne's straightforward mind, but the thought of Twitchell and Cotter shooting down two innocent people – Paul's parents – and then *firing* the place, was so utterly revolting as to make her feel physically sick.

She thought back, too, on that simple and unexplained sentence of Red's when he had told Widgeon, 'The girl Sarah was already in town,' and the thought came, intuitively rather than through any careful and logical deduction, that Red Twitchell had even engineered *that!*

Her full lips thinned down as jealousy, in spite of the horror within her, beat its mocking tattoo on her heart. Red was making a play for Sarah Escort! He had deliberately saved her from the killing at the Escort ranch – *saved her for himself*, Corinne thought bitterly.

She wondered then what Paul and the

marshal would do. Red had said they had returned to town and had probably seen the 'mess.' Talk was circulating that the marshal was fixing to organise a posse. That must mean that neither Paul nor Toomis knew who were the real perpetrators of this crime. Maybe they figured it was the work of Apaches or a few desperadoes, burning leather for the border, who robbed and pillaged for money and horses!

Corinne shaped and lit a quirly and wondered what she should do. Would it be any good in going to Toomis or even Paul and telling what she knew? Would the marshal consider her word on this overheard conversation suitable as *evidence?* For Corinne knew enough to understand that a good lawyer might well proclaim such 'evidence' as hearsay and, therefore, inadmissible!

There was another thought which struck her now, sending a cold shiver right through her body. She was in possession of dangerous knowledge, whether or not it could be used to incriminate Red, Jack Cotter and Charlie Widgeon. That meant that if any of them found out that she had eavesdropped on that conversation, then *her* life would not be worth a plugged nickel!

The more Corinne Devereux thought about it, the more she decided to do nothing – for the moment, at least – until she had time to figure the thing out clearly.

It looked now, she thought, as though this hideous crime were only a side issue, the main thing being the movement of a herd – Hackamore's cattle. She saw the plan now for what it was, simple and yet utterly ruthless.

In order to steal Hackamore's cattle and haze them south along the desert, they had first of all tried to *buy* the Escort place, and when that had failed Red and some others had ridden there and killed, thus obviating the possibility that the Escorts might see or hear the rustled herd go by at night. And this, Corinne reminded herself sharply, was due to happen *tonight!*

She knew that she had no way of leaving the Yucca to warn Hackamore, even had she wanted to – not without attracting immediate attention. Widgeon would be after her before even she had a chance to rent a horse from the livery, let alone get out of town. No, Corinne thought, there was no percentage in even *thinking* along those lines, and in any case Hackamore, big and powerful as it was, should be capable of looking after its own.

She was not over-concerned with that aspect of the situation. The shock of Red's horrible deed still held her in its grip, and yet, though she reviled herself bitterly, she could not rid herself of the burning wave of jealousy – jealousy at Sarah Escort – younger and prettier than herself...

Paul rode slowly back to Hackamore across the moon-silvered range. He was tired from long hours of riding, yet the ache in his limbs was slight in comparison with the dull, gnawing pain at his heart.

But over all lay a feeling of quiet thankfulness that at least Sarah had been spared the dreadful death which someone had meted out to his parents, almost, it seemed, with a wicked and complete absence of purpose.

He considered deeply the question which had been in both his own and Rich Toomis's mind; the first flickering suspicion against Red Twitchell, who had tried to buy the Escorts out. And Paul pounded his brain as to the *why* of this, if Twitchell were indeed guilty of such a crime.

Escort felt that somewhere, not far away, lay the solution to this problem; yet it continued to elude him. What good were a few acres of grass to a big syndicate anyway, even supposing Twitchell *was* an agent for a big combine?

And then the thought came that even if this *were* Twitchell's method of trying to gain possession, the killing and the burning did not make one iota of difference, because, even without a will having been left, *the Law would rule that the place now belonged jointly to Sarah and Paul!*

That being so, what could Twitchell or any man gain by this seemingly pointless and brutal crime?

At any rate, Rich Toomis was going to watch Twitchell and Cotter from here on out, as much as possible, and tomorrow the marshal had promised to ride out again in case some of the geldings had returned.

So soon, it seemed to Paul Escort, the Hackamore buildings showed up down in the dip. He could see lights burning in both bunkhouse and ranchhouse and felt a mild relief that he had not arrived back with everyone in bed and asleep.

He owed them that, at least, as he had been allowed time off to go home. If Frank had not yet returned, then he supposed he would have to tell Rona – Mrs Kearney, he corrected himself quickly.

Evidently she had heard the strike of shoes on gravel, for she appeared in the lighted doorway before Escort had ridden clear across the yard.

Now, Paul neck-reined the animal towards the hitch-rail and stepped from the saddle, waiting with his natural reticence as she descended the gallery steps and stopped within a few feet of him.

Paul touched his hat and murmured a greeting. In the strong light of the moon, Rona Kearney could see that his face was set in harsh lines. He looked older, yet his eyes seemed not to have changed. She wondered at that, for it was obvious that something had happened.

'What is it, Paul?' she asked softly.

He told her then, in a simple, unelaborated style, yet choosing his words carefully and not at once confiding in her with regard to his suspicions.

Horror, pity and anger reflected themselves in sequence in her rain-grey eyes as he concluded his telling of the tragedy.

'Come on up into the house, Paul,' she said at last, catching hold of his arm.

'Is Frank back yet, Mrs Kearney?'

Her eyes searched his face for the significance of his question. She shook her head. 'No, he's not back yet. But this is something which cannot be discussed out here. Maria will fix you some coffee. You look like you could use some.'

He followed her in then, amazed again at the size of the big living room, particularly now as it was empty of people except the two of them.

In a moment she had summoned the Mex girl, and a little while afterwards Maria brought in the freshly brewed coffee. Escort felt sure he had never tasted anything quite so good.

Presently she said, 'What do you figure on doing, Paul? You have the whole of Hackamore behind you in this–'

'I'm very grateful,' he said softly. 'At the moment, we – that is, Toomis and myself – have precious little to go on. Suspicion is one thing, proof another. I guess,' he added slowly, 'I could tackle Twitchell at the point of a gun, but I don't figure him as the type of man to squeal, whatever his crimes, and thus we might well lose the others who must be in on this thing.

'Also,' Paul continued, 'the trail herd is nearly ready and Jed wants me to come along on this drive to Three Forks–'

'We could arrange for you not to go–' Rona said quickly.

Escort shook his head. 'I'll do my job, Mrs Kearney, and work something out.' He stepped from the room and emerged from the house, walking slowly towards the now-darkened bunkhouse.

CHAPTER XI

The Big Steal

It must have been soon after Paul reached Hackamore that the first ragged clouds started blotting out the stars to the west, and an hour or so later the moon was only visible at short intervals behind the thicker, scurrying rain-clouds.

A strong wind had sprung up and Red Twitchell sniffed the air with his thin nostrils and nodded appreciatively as he turned to Jack Cotter, Johnny Rideout and Cass Dickerson.

'Reckon it won't be long before we get rain,' he grinned at them, and swung his glance around to include the four riders behind. The tally was complete, he thought with satisfaction. No more than two riders at a time had left town, and thus they had all eventually made rendezvous here in the juniper stand, not more than three-four miles south of Lariat and the Rio Chico.

'How long afore we reach the herd, Red?' Dickerson asked. 'Time's movin' an' we got a big job on our hands.'

'Don't get to frettin', Cass,' Twitchell grinned. 'Jack's been riding around here a lot lately, and has found a nice quick trail which'll carry us plumb on to thet dog-leg section, right where the beef's bedded down.'

'Well,' Cass said, 'I ain't worried any, only it must be after twelve an' it looks like the going might be purty rough.'

'It won't take as long as you figger,' Twitchell said. 'We'll push our mounts hard, while we kin still see, before the rain comes. After that it'll be heavy goin', mebbe. You all got yore slickers?' It was a rhetorical question and he didn't bother waiting for an answer.

He fed steel to the chestnut and, with Cotter riding alongside, the two of them led the way southwards, the others thundering at their heels.

They were able to cover the first sixteen miles or so at a fairly good lick, pausing now and again, but only for a few moments, to give the horses a blow. But now the sky was darkening steadily, and only faint and intermittent star- and moonlight showed from time to time from behind the rain-laden clouds.

They pushed on and the first drops of rain came slanting in at them as hastily they donned slickers without halting their mounts.

Water began dripping off hat-brims and leather became coldly wet and uncomfortable. But these men were used to such discomforts; they were riders of the owlhoot trail, and often enough bad weather had been their ally. Each man in Red Twitchell's gang had good cause to appreciate how preferable *this* kind of night-riding was to the desperate, full-stretch gallops so inevitable when a sheriff's posse chased them through the night and into the dangerous light of dawn.

But in spite of the heavy spring downpour and the all-enveloping darkness, they made good time, as Twitchell had prophesied, thanks to Cotter's recently discovered trail, which arrowed straight to their goal.

They drew rein at last in the shadow of a big rock outcropping, a mud-bespattered, evil and ruthless band, trained in the arts of stealing and killing.

Twitchell searched their faces in the gloom, which now, for a time at least, seemed to have lessened somewhat.

'Jack,' Twitchell said, 'you know where the line cabin is. Sure enough on a night like this you'll find the relief guards inside in the dry. You take Johnny and Makely with you. That oughta be enough to settle things at the cabin?'

'Sure,' Cotter grunted.

'All right. I'm ridin' with Pursloe around the herd from right to left. Cass'll start ridin' the *other* way at the same time with Heckmann. That way we'll intercept the two night-hawks ridin' herd. Whitey'll keep a lookout an' warn us should anyone happen along, but I don't figger that's likely.

'We'll give you a half-hour start, Jack, as you an' Johnny and Makely'll have farther to ride than us. Soon as you've finished, make fer the herd, but come up quietly and *sing out yore names fer Pete's sake!* Is that clear?'

Cotter nodded and said, 'Okay, Red, we're on our way.'

Their eyes were by now so accustomed to the night that they could see each other with partial clarity. The rain had eased off almost completely and some of the clouds had thinned out.

Red watched as the three men became swallowed up in the night. He hefted a pint whisky bottle from his *alforja* pouch and passed it around to each of the others. They grinned and smacked their lips and felt good in spite of damp clothes and rivulets of water running down their necks. The whisky helped the half-hour to run itself out fast.

Soon after they left the shelter of the outcropping they heard the restless, indefinable murmur of sound which always betokens the presence of a large herd of cattle. Then, a few steers raised isolated voices, bawling plaintively in the night, and Red Twitchell reined in, motioning the others to do likewise.

He peered ahead through the lightening night and made out, with difficulty, the dark mass of shapes which was Hackamore's herd for the loading pens at Three Forks.

Twitchell turned then, signalling to Whitey to stay put and beckoning up Pursloe to his stirrup. Silently, Cass Dickerson pulled away with the man Heckmann.

No words were needed now, as each desperado knew what he had to do.

Four men were to be killed and a thousand head of cattle hazed to the border. It was as simple as that.

Twitchell was not worried about noise attracting attention. It was hardly likely that anyone other than the four Hackamore men would be abroad tonight at this isolated place. *And there was no need to worry about any interference from the Escort ranch!* He grinned wolfishly in the darkness as his hand closed over the butt of his gun.

He signalled Pursloe to lag behind, for, up ahead, Red had spotted the dim shape of a single horse and rider, slowly circling the huge bedded-down herd.

The man wheeled his mount quickly as his ears caught the soft hoofbeats on the wet grass. He was slicker-covered, like Twitchell, and he peered through the night, seeking to identify the newcomer as his saddle-pard and wondering, late in the day, how come Del was riding up *behind* him.

'That you, Del?' Matheus called, and Twitchell grunted and rode slowly up to him. It was too late by then for Matheus to do anything. His gun was underneath the buttoned-up slicker and even as he started to move, attempting to spur his horse at the last moment, he felt the crash of hard steel on his head. He reeled, half senseless, in the saddle. Another smashing blow knocked him from leather and George Matheus knew no more.

He didn't hear the man who had attacked

him call out softly to his accomplice; nor did he feel the keen-edged knife which took him sharp and quick in the throat as his life's blood gushed out and over his scarf and slicker...

A little over a quarter-mile from where George Matheus met his death, Hackamore's second duty rider was mildly surprised to hear the rapid beat of hoofs and to glimpse the shapes of two riders. His first thought was that Matheus and perhaps another ranch-hand were riding to impart some important news.

At night, and with a man covered from neck to boots in the universal slicker, it was well nigh impossible to identify an individual until he was within a few feet. But even so, something in the quiet approach of the newcomers rang a warning tocsin inside Del Richards' head.

He started to unbutton his slicker, slowly at first, and then with feverish haste as the first rider came on him.

Cass Dickerson wanted no gun-play for the same reason as Twitchell, because of the possibility of starting a stampede with the cattle. Thus, even when Cass had the edge on this man, his gun unlimbered, he hesitated to use it except as a club, and that meant getting in close, within easy reach, stirrup to stirrup.

Richards saw the full gleam of light running the length of the gun barrel. At the same time he realized he could never get his own Colt out fast enough. He did the next best thing by feeding steel to his pony, causing it to rear and then plunge forward with such sudden violence that Del almost became unseated himself. But his pony's forelegs struck into the breast of the other horse, and then the whole weight of Del Richards' mount struck Cass Dickerson's horse with a juddering impact. Cass fought to control his thrashing horse, to keep its head down and to hold it to an upright position. But such had been the force and unexpectedness of the Hackamore rider's terrific lunge forward that Cass Dickerson found his own mount going over. Barely was he able to free his feet from stirrups before his pony crashed to the ground, half on its rump and half on its side.

Already Heckmann was spurring forward, gun in hand, but somehow, in the confusion, he became baulked by the shadowy figure of Cass himself, climbing to his feet. Dickerson's pony, too, was up in a moment, and caused Heckmann's mount to swerve violently. By the time Heckmann could bring his mount under control, the Hackamore rider was a vanishing shadow in the night. They heard his mount's hoofs drumming out a tattoo and knew that they had lost him irrevocably.

Cass Dickerson swore obscenely as he caught the reins of his horse. 'Thet bustard's high-tailin' it to Hackamore with the news. We better find Twitchell an' get movin'–'

'Sure hope him and Pursloe made out all right. Cotter too.'

They were not left long in doubt, for continuing on around the circumference of the now restless herd, they came on Twitchell and Pursloe, with Whitey riding anxiously in to find out what the ruckus was about.

They exchanged stories briefly, and Twitchell swore bitterly at Dickerson's news that a Hackamore rider had gotten away.

'Riders comin',' Whitey murmured from the outskirts of the group. All of them drew their guns now. They would have to chance a stampede and shoot it out if these riders were Hackamore.

Trigger-fingers were a mite itchy right then, but luckily for Twitchell's owlhoots, Jack Cotter sang out softly but clearly. In a few moments they made out the dim shapes of Cotter, Johnny and Makely. Red said sharply, 'One night-hawk got away, Jack. How is it at the cabin?'

Cotter grinned, feeling pleased even though the rain had now started to come down more heavily.

'East as falling off a log, Red. Them two jaspers never knew what hit 'em, an' they've sure taken their last ride.' He said this in the same tone of voice he might employ in discussing the branding of a steer or a game of stud poker.

Twitchell nodded. 'Well, it was sure hopeless to try chasing after that guy on a night like this, and I guess it'll take him the better part of two hours to reach the ranch; another two at least before any riders'll be along here. We got four-five hours, but we better start gettin' busy.

'Jack and Johnny! You two cut out a lead herd and get 'em started. Makely! Cass! Ride at point when the critturs are on their feet. Keep 'em in tight and close and as fast movin' as possible. Pursloe and Heckmann ride flank; me and Whitely'll bring up the drag. Hurry it up now, we only got about four hours before it starts gettin' light, anyway.'

It was around two o'clock when Paul Escort, tired as he was, awoke in the darkness of the Hackamore bunkhouse. Instinctively he reached for the gun where his belt hung on a wall peg at the head of his bunk, wondering for a second what had awakened him.

Then he heard the drumming hoofs: a veritable rataplan as a rider rode at a breakneck pace towards the ranch.

In an instant, Escort had tumbled out of his bunk, calling to Segal and getting a lamp lit, carefully keeping it low and away from the window.

Jed called sleepily, 'What in hell's up, Paul?'

'Get dressed,' Escort grunted. 'Best rouse the others, too. Cain't you hear that rider comin', lickety-spit?'

The racing hoofs were loud enough for any man to hear now as Segal sat up and started pulling his boots on.

'No jasper rides a bronc like that, 'specially at night, without he's bringin' bad news! Hey! Wake up you fellers,' he called to the now stirring men. 'Somethin's up, an' we sure better be booted an' spurred! Get out into the yard and bring yore guns with you!'

The bunkhouse crew was a depleted one right now, because four were night-hawking on the dog-leg holding grounds and three were nursing the gather choused from the brakes and bottomlands of the Rio Chico. But Slim Massey, Crick Rowland, Jim Grundy and A.B Roper were there, besides Paul and Segal himself...

Someone else had heard those urgent, racing hoof-beats in the night. Rona Kearney, stirring restlessly in the big double-bed, sat up suddenly as the noise slammed against her ears through the open window of her room.

It would be Frank, she thought, it *must* be

Frank, returning for some reason in the middle of the night!

She groped for sulphur matches and lit the bedside lamp with fingers that shook a little. She saw the time from the pocket watch lying on the table as being twelve minutes after two. She thought, *Here it comes. This is the payment I must make for marrying Frank in order to destroy him!*

She heard the rider's horse hit the hard-packed earth and gravel of the yard and heard the challenging voice of Segal, her – Frank's – ramrod. There were other voices of the crew, as well, and once she thought she heard Paul Escort speak in his quiet and modulated voice.

She felt an odd, utterly incomprehensible lift of spirits as she thought how alert these men were, even after hard riding all day. She felt for a moment as though they were *her* crew and that their tough loyalty and alert-ness was, in some obscure way, a compli-ment to herself. Then she recalled that they were Frank's men, all of them, whose loyalty and gun-handiness was bought with Frank's gold. All of them, that was to say, with the possible exception of Escort!

She arose now and thrust her feet into moccasins, throwing a warm wrapper about her night-clad form, tying the cord before descending the stairs and unlatching the wooden screen doors.

She came out into the cool night and felt the damp strike of rain-washed air. It was dark, but not pitch-black, for already the moon was beginning to peep through the scudding clouds. She realized, without even thinking deeply about it, that there must have been some heavy rainfall which had probably accounted for her restlessness.

Then she saw that the lathered horse in the yard was not one of Frank's, neither was the man standing in the group of ranch hands Frank Kearney, but one of Hackamore's riders.

She called out then, from the gallery, and startled a little by her sudden appearance the men hesitated before moving slowly towards her. She noticed, subconsciously, that it was Escort who was the first to move, and then the others followed.

They stood at the base of the gallery steps looking up at her with a kind of reluctant admiration.

These men did not work for Rona Kearney. Frank was their boss, yet immediately Jed Segal decided that they owed the same loyalty to this woman as they did to Kearney himself, more, perhaps, in the latter's absence, because Frank would hold them responsible.

'We got bad news, ma'am,' Jed told her. 'Del Richards jest come in on a spent horse from the dog-leg section–'

'Dog-leg section?'

'Yeah,' Segal explained patiently, 'the most southerly part of Hackamore where we bed down herds ready fer trail-drives. You tell it, Del,' Segal instructed.

Rona moved her eyes from the ramrod's face, settled her gaze on Escort's face for a second and then looked at Richards.

'What is it, Del?' she invited.

'Well, ma'am,' Richards explained, still a mite breathless, 'Matheus an' me was spellin' Forbes an' Dreizel with the big herd we done hazed down to the dawg-leg holdin' grounds. Everythin' seemed right peaceful, but it was rainin' an' plumb awful dark.

'Suddenly I heerd riders an' made out the shape of a man on a horse. I couldn't see nothin' much until he was almost atop me; him bein' slickered like me, I figgered at fust it must be one of us, either George Matheus or Forbes or Dreizel, but then I saw the gun in his hand. Thet hombre was sure tryin' to get in close an' club me with the gun–'

'If he *were* an enemy, a rustler, perhaps, why do you figure he didn't shoot you there and then, Del?'

They seemed a little surprised at such a penetrating question from a woman, but Richards answered promptly enough.

'I didn't think anythin' about that at that moment, but I sure had a heap o' time to figger it out on the ride back here. I reckon

178

I was plumb lucky to 've escaped, but I'm guessing that the others have been – killed!

'An' it musta been done purty quiet on account they didn't want to alarm the herd–'

'You mean, if there had been shooting,' Rona suggested, 'the herd might 've stampeded?'

Richards nodded. 'Sure–'

'Then,' Rona interrupted, 'you figure the herd is being stolen?'

Richards swallowed hard and nodded. 'That's what I got to thinkin' about on the ride back here. There wasn't nothin' I could do single-handed, an' I only got away by ridin' into the feller with the gun an' up-seatin' him. I dug in spurs *pronto* an' expected to get a shot in the back any second, but they was either in a jumble or else scared to start any shootin'.'

'They?' Rona Kearney said. 'I thought–'

'Yes, ma'am,' Del said. 'I saw another rider behind the fust one, but he couldn't get at me on account of his pard was between me an' him. I'm feered that they jumped Matheus as well, an' mebbe the boys in the line shack.'

'How many head of cattle were down at the – dog-leg section?' Rona asked, turning to Segal.

Jed scratched his head, though he knew the answer easily enough.

''Bout eight-nine hundred head o' prime stuff, Miz Kearney, an' a few mavericks we ain't branded yet. I'd say that tally was over a thousand head altogether.'

She said in a curiously level voice, 'Do you think rustlers would try to move the whole of that herd, Jed, and if so, where would they drive them?'

Segal shrugged slightly. 'They *could* rustle the whole shebang, I guess, if they was enough riders and they knew their job. As to *where*, why, I guess we'll have to get on over there an' see if we kin pick up any sign.'

Escort spoke then for the first time. 'If we ride out now, we'll be able to reach the section by first light. We can take it from there.'

Rona nodded thoughtfully. 'Wait, though. You'll need as many men as you can muster. Hadn't one of you best ride to the river brakes and bring in the men night-hawking there?'

Again the crew was surprised, particularly Escort and Segal. They wondered how it was that this new bride-wife knew so much about the workings of the ranch and cattle.

Segal felt a quickening of interest rather than any resentment at Rona Kearney's ability to ask direct questions and make such practical and knowledgeable suggestions.

He said: 'I guess that's a good idea, Miz Kearney. One of us'll ride over an' pick up

Darnell, Steve an' Butch. Meanwhile we'll be saddling up an' getting fresh mounts ready for the boys coming in.'

Rona nodded. She nearly suggested that Segal should roust out the cook for coffee and grub which they might well need on the ride, but she recollected herself in time. *That* sort of suggestion would be received in contemptuous silence by men who had spent their lives, off and on, night-riding, tracking and fighting to hold their own.

Indeed, there was nothing that savoured of incompetence or lack of experience in the way Segal issued his terse orders to the waiting men.

Rona went back inside and, once in her room, started to dress. There would be no more sleep that night for anyone, and her mind was now wide awake and active with conflicting thoughts.

A big steal, such as this, with a few more, perhaps, later on, might well bring a man even as powerful as Frank to the brink of ruin. True, his credit was good, both in Lariat and Sage Flats, the county town, but that was merely because he ran so many thousand head of carefully bred cattle. Take away a rancher's stock and the man becomes a pauper overnight!

That might be as good a way of breaking Kearney as any, she reflected, and shuddered a little in the cold pre-dawn gloom...

CHAPTER XII

Strange Welcome Home

The man Frank Kearney had been called upon to identify – the man who had been the unwitting means of dragging Kearney, figuratively, from the arms of his bride – *was not Jesse Evans!*

The Hackamore owner, as was his way, had sworn and stamped and blustered with the county officials and lawmen, accusing them of stupidity, incompetence and – the worst crime of all – that of wasting Frank Kearney's time!

But it was not so simple as that, as events had quickly proved. And those ensuing events had shown, quite positively, that although the captured man was not Jesse Evans, he was indeed an associate of Bonney and Evans, and had ridden with them at least once, on a horse-stealing raid. This, coupled with the fact that the man who gave his name simply as Curly was similar in build and looks to the redoubtable Evans, had resulted in the quite understandable mistake which Sheriff Commart had made.

It was a blunder, however, only in so far as

it was a case of mistaken identity, for the fact that Curly was as guilty of the crime for which he was accused as his two notorious accomplices was something that the Law in Sage Flats intended to prove.

The trouble and delay, as far as Frank Kearney was concerned, lay in the fact that on hitting the county seat, neither Kearney nor Deputy Sheriff Locke were able to locate Commart.

Frank, impetuous and over-riding, had insisted on going to the jail in the courthouse straight away and have done with this tiresome business of identification. And so he did, for Locke saw no harm in that. The real friction started when Kearney, having positively stated – and even written it down – that the prisoner was *not* Jesse Evans, wanted to ride back to Lariat there and then.

But Locke, for all his easy-going ways, showed a sudden hard and obstinate side to his nature. He argued that only to Commart himself could Kearney swear his statement. There was an added and stronger reason for Locke 'holding' Kearney until the sheriff should return, and this the deputy had explained as the two Franks glared at each other in the sheriff's office.

'I just had a word with the mayor, Mr Kearney,' Locke had grunted, seating himself at Commart's desk, 'an' it seems like Sheriff

Commart's picked up some information concerning Bonney and Evans. Seems like they may be hereabouts according to our tip-off, an' the sheriff's taken out in the hopes of nailin' them. That bein' so, Commart'd still want you here when and if he brings 'em in.

'You see, Mr Kearney, like I said before, we got Billy's description an' likeness plastered around, but we ain't so sure of Evans.'

Frank had made a real effort then to curb his temper, and the fierce impatience which had ridden him since this had all started.

'How long is it going to be before Commart *does* return?' he asked.

Both of them, red-eyed from loss of sleep and weary from miles of hard riding, sat slumped in their chairs.

'Don't figger it'll be over long,' Frank Locke opined, 'mebbe tonight, mebbe tomorrow. But you got my word for it that we'll settle this business *pronto*, just as soon as the sheriff rides in. Now, I guess we could both do with some sleep. Why don't you have a meal an' book a room at Democrat House? It's a good place, not over a hundred yards down street from here.'

'I think I will,' Kearney had said, and for the first time grinned in friendly fashion. There was an irony about this whole thing and Frank had suddenly, though belatedly, seen the wry humour in the situation. He wondered how many bridegrooms had spent their first two-three wedding nights away from their wives...

Thus, Kearney quit fighting the inevitable and resigned himself to the situation, eating well and sleeping in comparative comfort for most of the remainder of that day.

Commart didn't show up at night, but by that time Kearney had gotten into a poker game at the Sage Flats saloon and was steadily piling up for himself a stack of chips. He was feeling pretty spry now and Lady Luck seemed to be making amends for her cavalier treatment of his comforts earlier on.

He finished up some seven hundred dollars to the good, and although he considered it little more than chicken-feed, it had the advantage of making him feel good. He had not lost his ability to play a good poker game, it seemed, and to know when to bluff. Even the thought of the old wives' tale about 'lucky at cards, unlucky at love,' did not have the power to spoil his new-found good humour, nor his night's sleep – what was left of the night!

Sheriff Nat Commart rode into Sage Flats just after noon of the following day, and the whole town, it seemed, turned out to glue their avid gazes on the handcuffed prisoner who dejectedly sat the lead horse.

There was a ripple of disappointment as

soon as it was realized that this man was almost certainly Jesse Evans and *not* the fabulous William Bonney.

Somehow or another, though the information upon which the Law had acted had been reliable, Billy the Kid had miraculously escaped, and Evans denounced his companion bitterly, claiming that Bonney had left him, Jesse, to face the music by a trick, and that the yellow-bellied son had ridden away hell for leather on a fast horse for points west.

By the time all the fuss and excitement had simmered down a little it was early afternoon before Kearney's chance came and Frank was escorted over to the courthouse by Commart and Locke.

'You'll see now, Kearney, that from a distance at least Evans and Curly are sure enough alike. We figured we had Jesse first off, but we know now it's another of Bonney's pick-ups who–'

'But does Bonney run a gang of outlaws now?' Kearney asked.

Commart shook his head. 'We don't figger he runs with a bunch, it's mainly jest him an' Evans, but now and agin he lets someone ride along who he figgers will mebbe prove useful.'

They went inside the courthouse, passing the sheriff's office and turning down the passage which led to the cells.

It didn't take long for Kearney to satisfy both himself and the Law in Sage Flats that *this* time the prisoner was indeed Bonney's saddle-partner, Jesse Evans.

Curly was still in the adjoining cell, and thus Kearney had a good chance to compare likenesses. He was forced to admit that there was more than a fleeting resemblance. It was a mistake that anyone might have made, particularly as accurate descriptions of Evans had been hard to come by.

For his part, the outlaw continued to alternate between moods of sullen dejection and fierce vituperation directed mainly against Bonney.

Commart chuckled. 'It shore looks like that damned rat would sell his own brother. He's left Evans and Curly to face the music, without a doubt–'

'Yo're damned right he has, Sheriff,' Evans growled from behind the bars of his cell. 'An' we gotta take the rap fer all *his* crimes, I suppose–'

'If you mix with skunks you must expect to pick up some of the stink,' Commart grated. 'Now shut up an' keep quiet if you expect to get any food an' drink.'

'Well, there's no doubt about it *this* time, Sheriff,' Kearney confirmed as they retraced their steps and paused at the office door. 'That's Evans sure enough, and this time you got him safe. No dramatic rescues from

187

the stage, like the last time–'

'No,' Commart chuckled. 'And many thanks, Kearney, for coming here. I reckon now you'll wait till morning and catch the eight o'clock stage back, huh?'

'I'll haveta wait till morning,' the Hackamore owner agreed, 'but as I want to get my own horse back from the relay station, I won't be using that damned bone-shakin' coach…'

In the night the faint boom of a cannon sounded, and Kearney stirred in his bed and sleepily wondered who was celebrating the fourth of July so early. Before he had time to elaborate this train of thought he was asleep again and did not waken until the night clerk, going off duty, knocked at his door to rouse him, as instructed.

The man, hoping perhaps for another tip from this wealthy Rio Chico rancher, and eager to impart his news, opened the door, thrusting a cup of steaming java into Frank Kearney's hand.

Frank started to drink with noisy relish and gusto, and only stopped when the clerk said, 'Have you heard the news, sir? They's been big doings during the night! Seems like Billy the Kid didn't ride away at-all like Evans claimed, for the outside wall of the jail's been plumb blown away and there's nary a sign of Evans or Curly–'

'*What?*'

'It's true enough, Mr Kearney, sir. I was on duty all last night, as you know, and along about two o'clock I heard this almighty roar an' ran to the door. Presently I saw the sheriff an' deputy Locke racin' over to the courthouse–'

'But don't they sleep there,' Kearney demanded, 'in the sheriff's office?'

'No sir! Not Frank Locke an' Nat Commart – they got cottages, but they *was* a deputy in the jail, of course. Seems that he'd been slugged pretty hard with a pistol barrel an' tied up, an' like I said, half the wall was blown out from back o' the cells an' the desperadoes had gone!'

'What does Commart figure happened then?' Kearney asked, thankful that now Evans had been identified this latest development was not likely to interfere in any way with Frank's return to Hackamore.

'Well, sir, he wouldn't say much to me or the other folks as had heard the noise and come out to see what the ruckus was. But he sure was hoppin' mad, an' I heard him telling Locke how Bonney musta outsmarted them agin an' that Evans's talk about Bonney ridin' out an' leavin' them had been so much dust thrown in their eyes.'

'Yeah,' Kearney said thoughtfully, 'I guess it must've been. Evans sure created the impression that Bonney was likely halfway across the territory by late yesterday.'

'Sure, Mr Kearney. That's just where he outsmarted them. Evan's talk was all a part of the plan to make them figger Billy had high-tailed out. 'Stead of which he was probably right close an' laughin' at them like the devil he is.'

Kearney fished for a cigar and lit it. It was full early as yet and he had ample time to dress and breakfast before lighting out on the horse loaned him by the county.

He pondered over this latest piece of news and for the life of him could not see how it would affect him in any way. Just so long as the outlaw trio didn't try stealing any of *his* horses or cattle, he wasn't much moved by the turn of events, although he'd have had no objection in seeing Evans strung up – the only one of the outlaws who had attempted to hit at Hackamore.

'Have the day clerk send up my bill,' Kearney told the man as he still stood by the door, reluctant to go. Frank threw back the bedclothes and padded across to the chair in his long underwear, fishing down into his pants' pocket and producing a couple of silver dollars.

He dropped them into the clerk's outstretched hand and the man nearly fell over himself with gratitude. 'I'll have your bill sent up right away, sir,' he promised, 'and I'll get the help to bring you hot water.' He closed the door as Kearney nodded abstractedly and began, slowly, to dress.

By the time Kearney was in the saddle, with a good breakfast under his belt, he had almost forgotten the incident of last night's dramatic jail-break. He had glimpsed the sheriff on the board-walk immediately before setting out, but Commart was a desperately worried and fuming man and had given Kearney few more facts than the clerk at Democrat House had done.

Kearney had shrugged. Maybe someone *would* nail Commart's hide for this, but it was no skin off Frank's nose.

But if he could have seen how last night's affair *was* going to affect him, *then Frank Kearney might well have been a badly rattled man...*

Once again, in characteristic fashion, William Bonney had played tag with the Law and had thumbed his nose at the efforts of the Peace Officers. His defiance was incredible, his actions often absurdly rash. Yet time and time again he got away with it! This New-York-born desperado, who had killed his first man at the tender age of twelve years, had ridden the trails from Silver City to Arizona, down into Mexico and northwards again through Texas. He was wild, ruthless and unpredictable and was an excellent shot as well as a superb horseman. Indeed, it was often his Comanche-like riding which enabled him so frequently to elude and outwit sheriffs' posses. He would kill without compunction, often with evident enjoyment, to avenge a fancied insult, to aid a friend or to plunder for gold which he promptly lost at the gaming tables.

And the grey horse of Billy the Kid was almost as much a legend as was its master himself.

This, then, was the man who plucked his friends from jail and shouted his defiance from the roof-tops; the man who now rode with Evans and Curly at his stirrup as dawn began to lighten the sky to the east of Sage Flats.

They drew rein in the shadow of a clump of cottonwoods, dangerously near to Sage Flats.

Curly said, 'Reckon we're too damned close, Billy; hadn't we oughta be ridin' hell for breakfast?'

And Bonney stroked his lean, black-stubbled jaw and laughed and said, 'That's just what they will think, Curly, isn't it? Commart's figgerin' that by now we're in the badlands, where he couldn't even trail us!

'Mebbe at that,' Bonney continued, 'we'll head for the Rio Grande, steal us some good horseflesh and push it across like we done before.'

'This is as good a time as any to say,

"Thanks, Billy,"' Evans said soberly. 'Mebbe if you wanta ride on a spell an' then wait three-four days for me you will. But I got a chore to do that no one else can do for me.'

They glanced at him sharply and then Bonney laughed again and turned to Curly. 'Jesse wants to take the hombre who put the finger on him. Ain't that right, Jesse?'

Evans nodded. 'I owe you enough already, Billy, without wantin' you hornin' in on this. You shore got me out of a fix last night, but I ain't sleepin' peaceful until I've lined my sights on thet bustard Kearney. That's right enough.'

Bonney sighed. 'Jesse,' he said, 'if it was anyone but you doin' all this fool talkin', I'd get impatient enough to blow 'em apart. As it is – well, I guess you gotta do what's on your mind. Curly an' me'll push on to the hide-out farm near San Mayo.

'We'll stick around there for a week, mebbe ten days. I guess if you're not along by then you won't be comin' at all!'

'That's fairly spoken, Billy,' Evans grunted, leaning forward in the saddle to shake his friends' hands.

They watched him for a while as he rode a wide loop clear of Sage Flats thirty miles away, preparatory to hitting the road along which Frank Kearney would have to travel.

Evans had not let on, in jail, that he even remembered this Rio Chico rancher from the time, way back, when Kearney and a few of his riders had jumped him before. But his hatred of the man had gone pretty deep then, for hitherto no one had even gotten a good enough look at Jesse to identify him positively. For that matter, no one *since* that time had done so. Only this bustard Kearney had been able to put the finger on him, and Jesse's old hatred for the man was as nothing compared with the flaming rage which possessed him now and was directed against the rancher.

Not only was this a case for vengeance from the point of view of a pleasurable chore, it was also a question of dire necessity. So long as Frank Kearney lived, so would he remain a ready witness on whom the Law could call any time. For the Law in Sage Flats had no time to get a tinplate made of Jesse nor even an artist to sketch his likeness. Billy had seen to that by his bold, fast action. And any good defence lawyer could cause doubt in a jury's mind by inferring that the Law was either prejudiced or downright mistaken in any future question of identity. But so long as Kearney was alive Commart or any other county sheriff would not have to ask the court to take *their* word for it. All they would have to do was to produce their Ace-in-the-Hole – Kearney!

But, for all his burning hatred, Jesse Evans resolved to temper retribution with caution.

He would trail this Kearney all the way, if a suitable opportunity to kill him did not present itself before!

And as Evans rode, keeping a wary eye cocked and utilizing whatever cover the terrain offered, he speculated as to whether Kearney would catch a stage from Sage Flats or whether he would make the long ride home forking a horse. Evans's guess was that the man would prefer to make his own way, at his own pace, aboard a horse. Few cattlemen cared overmuch for any other means of transport if it could be avoided. Still and all, if a coach appeared on the road, Jesse would have to make some excuse to stop it and glance inside, whatever the risk...

Frank Kearney, unaware that death stalked his heels, sighted the lights of Hackamore with a feeling of happy relief. He was tired, hungry and dust-covered, but he rode his own chestnut now and he was home and *Rona Kearney would be waiting for him!*

Weary as he was, he did not fail to notice the quiet, deserted air of the place; the complete absence of those familiar noises which are an integral part of a ranch. Certainly the lamps were lighted in the house, but now he saw that the bunkhouse seemed dark and empty. It came to him then that the whole crew was out, and sudden anger had its way for a moment. Yet, he could scarcely believe that Segal would sanction such a thing just because the boss was away!

Well, he would soon know. He left the horse at the hitch-rail and strode into the house and through into the living room, where he hauled up abruptly, anger, amazement, incredulity crossing his beefy face as he gazed at his wife, standing with her back to the fireplace *and holding a levelled gun in her hand pointing directly and unwaveringly at his belly!*

'My God! – Frank!' she gasped, and for a moment he thought she would swoon. He came towards her, ignoring the pistol, which she had now lowered, and caught her in his arms, smothering her mouth and throat with kisses, eager to participate in that which had been snatched away from him three days ago. So eager as to let explanations wait.

But firmly, now, she pushed him away, trying to hide the revulsion she felt at his crude handling of her.

But, impatient as he was, he knew well enough that something was amiss, and, characteristically, he assumed that her distraught condition – the pistol, everything – was the result of this something which had happened prior to his arrival.

'What is it, Rona?' he demanded. 'What's going on here, and why the gun pointed at me the moment I came in? Goddamit, woman, you've got some explaining to do.

196

Speak up, will you?'

Desire had given way to righteous anger, and now he was impatient in another way; impatient for an explanation of his wife's amazing behaviour.

He could see that she was pale, and without further word he crossed to a side table and sloshed whisky into two glasses. He handed her one and said: 'Now then, Rona, drink that up and pull yourself together and tell me what's happened.'

She drank slowly at first and then with an almost reckless abandon, taking a sudden delight in the bitter, unfamiliar bite of the liquor.

She said, colour slowly returning to her cheeks, 'The herd's been stolen, Frank. The herd that was bedded down on the dog-leg section. At least, that's what we figure—'

'Stolen?' Frank could do no more for the moment than to ejaculate that one horrified word and continue staring at her open-mouthed, as though she were crazy.

She nodded. 'The whole crew's been out since first light. Del Richards came in early morning with the news that he was attacked by unknown riders. He figures Matheus and maybe the men in the line-cabin were similarly attacked. We – that is Segal and the others and myself – feared that the men may be dead – killed – so that rustlers could move that trail herd!

'I – I thought when I heard your horse, Frank, it was someone – oh, I don't know – more trouble! There's no one here except myself and Maria, so I picked up the gun–'

She broke off, horror dilating her eyes and choking her words as she glimpsed the shadowy figure through the window pane. She had no more than a vague impression of a man's face, shaded by the down-drawn hat brim, and a long-barrelled Colt glinting in his upheld hand.

Just for that moment Frank had taken his eyes off her long enough only to refill his glass. And in that brief measurement of time Rona Kearney saw a quick and perfect solution to her long months of planning.

Outside on the porch someone was waiting to draw a bead on Frank and kill him. All she had to do was to keep Frank's attention riveted on herself and away from the window. The unknown man outside would do the rest; rid her of an unwanted husband and revenge her for Steve's death!

CHAPTER XIII

Rona Kearney's Choice

Frank stood spraddle-legged in the centre of the vast room, the replenished glass in his hand.

Rona, with a supreme effort, had dragged her gaze from the window. Her eyes no longer betrayed her, and to some extent she had the whisky to thank for that. She could feel it coursing through her body, revitalizing her and laying its fiery yet sedating touch on her brain.

Her thoughts seemed to come even more quickly now and with a greater, needle-sharp clarity than before. The idea came to her that she was being called upon to make a choice. At first she resisted the gentle voice of conscience, but then she realized suddenly, *If I do nothing, then I am myself a killer – a murderess!*

Horror griped her again, almost as it had done when she had first glimpsed that shadowy figure through the window, but a horror now directed inwardly at herself. It was as though she stood on the brink of a deep ravine, contemplating self-destruction, only to draw back in the nick of time as she felt the edge crumbling under her feet.

She whirled suddenly, bringing up the gun and cocking it simultaneously with levelling it at the window.

'*Look out, Frank! The window!*' she screamed, and fired deliberately at the glass, shattering it to fragments. The gun's roar sent reverberating echoes around the room; smoke curled up from the Smith and Wesson's barrel. Frank had whipped round into a half-crouch, his own gun drawn now and thrusting forward, his face, for all its normal fullness, honed down to a fine degree by the very breathless moment: the frightening nearness of sudden and unexpected death.

He fired, and his shot sent the remaining slivers of glass from the window frame. There was no answering fire from outside, and for an arrested moment neither of them knew whether their shots had gone home.

Belatedly, Frank blew out the table lamps before turning to the door, naked and smoking gun in hand.

Then the sound of racing hoofs hit their ear drums, near at first, but fast receding into the night.

Rona, still clutching the gun, smiled. Her face was chalk white. 'Whoever it was, he's gone now, Frank,' she said, and quietly sank to the floor, the gun falling from her numbed fingers.

It was a few seconds before the fact could penetrate Kearney's bludgeoned brain that Rona was neither dead nor even hit. He remembered dimly that there had been no answering shot.

He looked around him wildly, and then, awkwardly at first, lifted his wife and placed her upon one of the big leather sofas, only aware then that he still held the gun in his hand.

He holstered it and crossed to the liquor table, his own glass, which he had dropped, crunching into the carpet under his boots. He half-filled fresh glasses and carried them across the room, setting the one down and placing the other to Rona's lips.

He half-supported her head and shoulders in the crook of his arm, feeding her a little of the spirit in the light of the fire and the hanging lamps which he had had no time to douse.

A little colour swam into her waxen cheeks and presently her eyes fluttered open. For a moment she seemed not to recognize him. Then memories crowded back and her glance moved over to the shattered window.

She returned her gaze to Frank's anxious face, and wondered why she should feel so revolted by his almost brutal masculinity.

Was it because she feared the natural consequences of marriage, or was it because, deep down inside her, she still hated

Kearney, body and soul, for what he had done to Steve?

She was not so sure of the answer now as she had been before the shooting. And she had no ready answer within herself as to why she had saved his life, when, by merely stepping aside, she could have solved everything; no answer other than the feeling of horror she had experienced at the thought that she would have been as guilty as the man outside, all set to pull the trigger.

At least Frank would not expect her to submit to his attentions; not tonight! And even if he did, the whisky was helping to smooth away her panic and fear. She almost laughed aloud when she considered what Frank's reactions would be if he had to carry his wife upstairs, dead drunk!

But there was to be no need for such thoughts to disturb the now near-tranquil surface of her mind and being. For, within the hour, the rataplan of hoof-beats from a cavalcade of riders proclaimed the return of the crew – with their long-awaited news...

In the yard, Jed Segal lifted his tired gaze to the men around him.

'You've all been in the saddle since first light and need food and rest. Get the cook to rustle you up a meal and then...' His gaze flitted to the blanket-draped bodies lashed to the spare horses.

Crick Rowland, his voice cracked with

strain and anger, said: 'We'll see to buryin' them, Jed, jest as soon as we've unsaddled.'

One of the riders laid his glance on the hitch-rack across the yard. 'Looks like Frank's back,' he said. 'That's his hoss, ain't it?'

In answer the screen door opened and Kearney's solid bulk showed, silhouetted against the lamp-light behind.

Segal let go a deep sigh, half-relieved, half-anxious. 'Yeah. That's Frank.' He turned then to Escort. 'You better come in, Paul, and say your piece, since you found the boys in the line-cabin.'

Escort nodded and followed the ramrod towards the house. Already Frank had hailed them, and Segal lifted his hand in acknowledgement. In a moment or two they were all inside the big living room, Paul and Jed both gazing curiously at Rona lying on the sofa, and then transferring puzzled glances to the shattered window.

Frank said grimly: 'I'll tell you what happened here afterwards.' He crossed to the small table, pouring drinks for the new-comers.

'Now, Jed. Let's have it fast!'

Segal took a quick sip and then launched into his story.

They had found that all but a handful of cattle had been driven off and, like Del Richards had feared, Matheus was dead; hit over the head and stabbed to death!

Rona's face paled a little, again, but the unaccustomed whisky she had drunk had toughened her so that after the first shock of Jed's news she listened almost calmly. Not so Frank, who paced the room with a restlessness that indicated the measure of his angry frustration.

Paul told briefly how he had ridden over to the line-cabin with two of the hands and had found both the night-hawks stabbed to death, just like Matheus. There was nothing they could do for the men beyond blanket-wrap them and bring them back for burial.

'This knifing a man to death seems out of character with cattle thieves,' Paul said, 'until you consider that they were possibly anxious not to spook the cattle with gunfire.'

Kearney nodded. 'You followed tracks?' he asked, turning back to Jed.

'We had *some* sign to follow, for a way, but it rained here last night, Frank, purty hard at times. We had a tough job finding anything, but we did get as far as the desert–'

'The desert, eh?' Frank gritted. 'That means the thieves hazed the stuff around or across the desert to the border. It means, Jed, there's no chance in hell of getting them back?'

Segal shifted his feet, uncomfortably aware that Kearney was right and that this steal represented a pretty big loss, even to Hackamore. Not only was it a question of numbers, over a thousand head, but most of that trail-drive stuff was prime stock.

They all started suddenly at the sound of Rona's low voice. She had not spoken until then, and still lay with head and shoulders pillowed on the sofa. Her eyes were narrowed as she looked from Paul to her husband.

'That isn't everything, Frank,' she said. 'Yesterday, Escort rode south to his parents' ranch. He found the place in ruins and his folk dead–'

'*What?*' Frank slewed round and slumped into a chair. 'What the hell has been happening here?' He turned then to Paul. 'I'm damned sorry, Escort. Anything that Hackamore can do will be done! But how long have them damned red-devils been on the warpath. I ain't heard–'

Paul said softly, 'We don't think it was Indian work, Mr Kearney. Toomis found tracks which had been made by white men–'

'White men? By God, Escort, we'll–' Suddenly he stopped. A dawning light showed in his eyes. Deliberately he put his glance on each of them in turn.

'Don't you see?' he asked in a softly ominous voice. 'Don't you see the pattern of this devilish thing?'

He glanced back at his wife, who was now sitting erect on the big sofa. 'If what Escort says is true, I mean the way Toomis figgers it, then it looks like– By God! No! Even rustlin' renegades wouldn't–'

'I think they would, Mr Kearney,' Escort said in a flat voice. 'At first *I* couldn't believe what Toomis was suggesting; what he had in mind. But it fits like a dovetail joint. Whoever stole your cattle, Mr Kearney, was responsible for killing my parents and burning the ranch, *because the Escort place lies astride the trail to the border!*'

The silence which followed was thick and heavy, broken only by such small noises as a burning log falling in the hearth, the soft rustle of clothes as Frank reached for his glass and drained the contents.

'Hell, Paul,' Jed Segal breathed softly. 'I didn't know–'

Paul shook his head. 'You were all asleep when I got into the bunkhouse late last night. Since then' – he shrugged – 'there's been so much to do.'

Frank was viciously chewing on an unlit cigar. He raised his eyes to Paul's face.

'Suppose these two things *do* tie in, Escort, an' I think you're right about that; you got any idea–?'

Paul rolled a *cigarrito* and looked across at Rona. She nodded, giving him a brief smile.

'Marshal Toomis and I,' he said, 'agreed to give out the story that we figured this to be an Apache raid. Incidentally,' he went on,

206

remembering that the others did not know about Sarah, 'my sister was safe in town at the time—'

'Then she's – all right, Paul?' Jed asked, and Escort nodded.

'Red Twitchell got her away from the ranch, Mr Kearney,' Paul explained. 'Seems he wanted Sarah to model a dress for him at the dressmaking shop; a gown he wanted to send to his sister in Albuquerque—'

'My God,' Kearney growled. 'That was providential at least.'

'Twitchell offered us two thousand for my father's place only a few days ago,' Paul said sombrely, 'just for the buildings and a few acres of grass. Do you see anything in *that*, Mr Kearney?'

Frank suddenly jumped to his feet, his face dark with angry enlightenment. 'It's daylight clear!' he shouted. 'Twitchell wanted the place so that he could haze my critturs – mebbe other herds as well later on – past your ranch and south to the border. So long as you or your folks were there, there was a good chance the rustlers would be seen or heard, movin' a sizeable bunch like that! Jumping firecrackers,' he roared, clapping a big hand to his holstered gun. 'What are we waitin' for? Twitchell's not only our rustlin' bastard but a murderer to boot—'

'We haven't a shred of proof, yet,' Paul

said softly, and, in the ensuing silence, the sound of a fast-running horse came at them through the early night...

It was late afternoon and already the lamps had been lighted in the Yucca saloon. There were no more than a scattering of drinkers at the bar and a few early gamblers at the roulette table. The faro and monte lay-outs were not generally uncovered until later.

Corinne sat nursing a small drink in a particularly secluded booth. She had been restless all day, on edge and uncertain through the guilty knowledge she held.

She felt like a trapped animal, almost too scared to move. For, if Red should read that knowledge in her eyes, then she knew she would not have to worry about her future. It would be settled for her – a cold grave in boothill.

She shuddered at her thoughts, and, disillusioned as she was, discovered that she was not yet ready to die. She wanted desperately to live and chance what fate held in store for her. Even the bleak prospect of remaining here, or the possibility of lighting out for other parts, seemed brightly preferable to – dying.

She started violently, nearly spilling her drink, as spurred boots pounded the puncheon floor past her booth. She caught a fleeting glimpse of Red and Jack Cotter, both dust-covered and dirty, yet with a hint of triumph in their faces.

So they have taken the herd and have been paid, she thought, and wondered for a moment how and when the wrath of Hackamore would descend upon them.

She sat for a long time, undisturbed by anyone, frozen into an immobility which she seemed powerless to throw off.

Her mind told her that she ought to be in the dusty room upstairs, listening to the conversation in Charlie's office, through the knothole in the floor. Yet her limbs seemed not to heed the prodding of thoughts which, indeed, were too ineffectual to galvanize her body into positive action.

But at last, contemptuous of her own weakness, she gathered herself, not knowing quite what she would do. And then Red came through from Charlie's office, followed by Widgeon himself and Cotter.

She watched them belly up to the bar for a drink and noticed the restless mood of Twitchell. He kept glancing up at the clock over the bar and played around with his shot glass instead of swallowing the contents at a single gulp, as was his usual method.

Something impelled her then to slip quietly out from the booth on the other side, the side nearest the door which led to the stairs and rooms above. But, instead of ascending to her room, she slipped quietly through the rear door of the building and began picking her way carefully over the can-strewn and weed-grown lot towards the side alley.

There was some weird instinct playing its part in all this, and only afterwards did she realize the fact. At present she was almost like a sleep-walker, her actions directed by her subconscious rather than her conscious mind.

The cool evening air caressed her face as she rounded the corner of the building and froze suddenly at this end of the dim, shadowy alley. The nebulous, half-formed impulse which had brought her here – perhaps with the object of waiting at the head of the alley for Red to show up and then following him – disappeared like the morning mists as she heard the low voices and dimly, through narrowed eyes, made out the tall shape and the smaller one melting into it.

She leaned back against the clapboard wall, her eyes closed for a moment, half fearful to move and yet partly resigned to whatever would be. She even made the slightest sound as she shifted her feet on the rough ground, but the two lovers were oblivious of anything but themselves.

'In a little while, Sary,' Red was saying, 'we'll be all set to get married and shake the dust of this town from our feet. I got one-two more deals to make yet. Meanwhile, here's a few dollars to buy yourself some fancy duds an' a few gee-gaws–'

Corinne heard the slight gasp as Twitchell thrust the money into the girl's hand. And Corinne knew, without seeing or being told, that *gold* and not silver pieces exchanged hands in that darkened alley.

Gold, not silver! What difference did it make? It was still a Judas act, and although she hated Sarah Escort bitterly at that moment, Corinne knew deep down in her aching heart that Red Twitchell and not Sarah Escort was the betrayer.

Only fleetingly did she feel the pain, and then a hungry fury began to consume her so that she shook silently, her back still pressed against the clapboard behind her.

As from a far-off distance, she heard lovers' murmurings, rash promises for a bright future, and only a long time afterwards did she become aware that they had gone…

This, then, was the fork in the road which she had always half feared lay ahead of her. Here was the final dividing of the ways if she were to make her decisive choice. She could, she supposed, do just nothing about all this, but Corinne Devereux was not built that way.

The spasm of shaking rage passed, leaving her bitterly vindictive and ready, at last, to take positive action.

She made her way back through the rear door and ran swiftly upstairs, not pausing until she stood inside her own pitiful and tawdry little room.

Hurriedly she rummaged among her belongings, finally bringing to light an old pair of whipcord trousers, boots and a woollen shirt and a jacket; clothes which she had never donned since first riding into Lariat when it had been scarcely more than a tent town.

She paused to listen at the door of her room, but could hear nothing except the murmur of raucous voices and the clink of glasses from the saloon below.

She relied on the night and the early evening hour to reach the livery without attracting undue attention. As to what she was doing, folk were too preoccupied right then to speculate on it – until much later.

Harvey, the hostler, glanced curiously at her as she stood at the door of his office and made known her request. She wanted a good fast horse to rent and held gold in her hand to prove she meant business. Harvey shrugged and pocketed the twenty-dollar piece. It was not his business to question Corinne Devereaux, and, in fact, if she returned the horse without injury, there would be change to come for her out of that gold piece.

He saddled and bridled a rangy-looking

buckskin and shortened the girths to the girl's requirements.

'Thank you, Al,' Corinne smiled down at the liveryman. 'I won't mistreat the animal, and' – she paused for a moment – 'I'd rather you didn't mention this to anyone, Al–?'

He regarded her quizzically for a moment in the lamplit interior of the stables. Every-one in town knew she was Red Twitchell's woman, but that knowledge did not prevent oldsters like Al and the marshal and a few others from admiring this woman – from a distance! She was pretty enough with a shapely figure and, as far as they knew, had never done anyone any harm. On the con-trary, she had enlivened many an evening in the Yucca just by her presence, her readiness to share a joke or a drink without attempting to take them (at least the traders in Lariat) for a ride.

Al Harvey watched her gig the horse quietly and unobtrusively out on to the street until she became a shadowy, unidenti-fiable shape mingling with other riders. He scratched his head slowly, suddenly recall-ing the words he had used to himself a moment ago. She *had* enlivened many an evening, he had thought, as though it were now all over and done with!

He shook his head in mild perplexity and returned to his chair and paper in the office...

Meanwhile, once clear of town, Corinne Devereux gave the long-legged buck its head. She knew well enough whereabouts Hackamore lay, and once she had taken the right-hand fork of the road she was less worried about meeting stray riders who might consider her presence on the stage-road at night as something warranting an explanation.

Corinne Devereux was no range-girl, although she could ride, but the buckskin was trail-wise and seemed to know the destination its rider had in mind.

In a little under an hour Corinne sighted Hackamore's lamplit buildings in the dip. She put the buck to a fast run, not drawing rein until horse and rider clattered into the yard.

A little breathless and white of face, she slid from leather as the screen door opened and a man's shape showed itself for a moment. She caught the glint of light on metal and called out sharply, identifying herself.

Jed Segal relaxed and descended the gallery steps. He sheathed the six-gun and gave the girl a hard, questioning stare.

'Better come on up to the house, Miz Corinne,' he said shortly.

CHAPTER XIV

Shoot-out at the Yucca

She stood in the centre of the room, feeling a sudden stab of jealousy at Rona Kearney's richly gowned loveliness, and sadly conscious of her own masculine and almost disreputable appearance.

She thrust the thoughts and feelings aside, addressing herself to Frank and, to a lesser degree, Segal and Escort as well.

They offered her a chair, and gratefully she accepted the drink which Kearney passed her.

'You say you know all about this cattle loss of Hackamore, Miss Devereux?' Frank asked incredulously. 'I guess I don't understand. It only happened last night–'

Corinne waved an impatient hand. 'I overheard Twitchell planning this thing with Charlie Widgeon,' she interrupted. 'Cotter was there too. They are the ringleaders. Red's got some sort of undercover gang in town. Men he can call on for things such as this.

'I know, too,' she went on, looking at Paul and then dropping her gaze, 'that Twitchell and Cotter were responsible for that raid on the Escort ranch–' She broke off, waiting for the inevitable explosion to follow her verbal bomb.

But instead Paul said softly, 'Are you sure, Miss Corinne, that you actually heard Twitchell plan this thing with Widgeon and Cotter?'

'I only heard them planning to steal Hack-amore's cattle, stuff that'd been gathered and was bedded down on the dog-section. But they talked about the raid on the Escort ranch, and from the way they spoke I know it was – done by Red Twitchell and Jack Cotter–'

'But aren't you' – Segal hesitated – 'bespoken for by Red Twitchell?'

She lifted her tired, bitter gaze to the ramrod's face. Her smile was a travesty.

'Red is promising marriage to Sarah Escort, Paul's sister. That's something else I overheard, only tonight, not more than an hour – two hours ago. I seem to have spent all my spare time listening at keyholes–' Her voice trailed off and she drained the whisky glass in her hand.

'Looks like we got all the proof we want for the Law to step in now,' Segal suggested.

'The Law?' Kearney snarled. 'Since when has Hackamore quit fighting its own battles! We'll leave Toomis out of this – as far as the rustling is concerned, anyway. What Escort wants to do–'

'Toomis is a good man,' Paul said harshly, 'but he can keep out of this. And if anyone gets between me an' Twitchell–' He stopped and glanced curiously at the Hackamore owner. Without realizing it, he used Kearney's first name. 'If you're riding to town, Frank, I'll ride along with you. If you're not – I'll go alone!'

For the first time Rona swung her feet down from the sofa and stood up. She laid her compassionate gaze on Corinne's face. 'You realize what this means – Corinne?' she said. 'You realize that there will be a terrible fight, that men will be killed tonight, perhaps Twitchell, perhaps Frank – Paul – Jed–?'

Corinne nodded mutely. The fury and rage which had set her feet on to this road of retribution had receded again suddenly, leaving her with a weak and helpless feeling; pain made her features harsh, almost ugly, in the bright overhead lights.

'I would've backed Red all the way – for most things,' she said, speaking in a low voice. 'Even murder! But not – not murder like – like an Injun would do it! In any case – now it's finished. Red's making a play for' – she nodded her head towards Escort – 'his sister. And I hope Paul *kills* him and dam' his soul to hell, else Sarah Escort will find out, too late, what kind of a devil he is!'

217

'Where's Twitchell and Cotter and Widgeon now?' Frank demanded.

Corinne shrugged apathetically. 'In town, still, for sure. Probably in the Yucca–'

'What about *you?*' Rona asked, addressing the girl.

Frank said: 'She'd best stay here with you for the moment, Rona, at least until we get back.

'Jed! Get horses saddled for the three of us, we're ridin' in to finish this thing now!'

'You want the crew along, Frank?' Segal asked quietly, and Kearney's head came up with a jerk, nodding. 'They got a right to be in on this, Jed, considerin' they only jest got through buryin' three of their friends. But you an' me an' Escort'll go in – alone. I guess that's the way you both want it?'

Paul nodded, and Segal ground out, 'That's the way we want it, Frank!' He turned on his heel and stepped out of the room; they heard his bootfalls and the jingle of his spurs as he clattered down the gallery steps and moved across towards the crew's quarters.

Rona gazed at her husband, feeling a sudden wave of admiration. She resented experiencing such an emotion, but it would not be denied. Frank Kearney was the egotist supreme; never for a moment doubting his own judgment, his own capabilities. And not for a second did he doubt but that he would return later tonight, the hanging crime of rustling punished by the deaths of Twitchell, Widgeon and Cotter.

She knew that Frank could put the matter into the hands of Marshal Toomis, if he so wanted, and reference made to the county seat. With a sworn testimony from the girl, the Law could not be swung in favour of the thieves and killers!

Yet Frank would not even consider such a solution. He minded the time, way back, when Jesse Evans had escaped both Hackamore's brand of justice and the Law itself. And recently Evans had escaped again, along with Curly, the other owlhoot, thanks to Billy the Kid. Maybe the same thing would happen with Widgeon and Twitchell if the Law were invoked.

But the Law would not be brought into it this time. Frank shook his head vigorously as though to clear away lingering doubts. He only hoped Rich Toomis wouldn't go getting under their feet at the crucial moment!

He raised his head again as the sound of men and horses in the yard proclaimed that Jed had moved fast. Paul, sensing that Frank might well desire to bid his wife a passionate farewell, moved from the room and made his way out front. But, in a surprisingly short time, Frank emerged from the house and joined the men in the yard. For all his recent long hours of riding and the abortive attack on his life tonight, he looked spry as most younger men, and a good deal more dangerous.

'Slim and Del!' he called to the silently gathered group. 'Someone's gotta stay here and look after my wife and Corinne Devereux. Keep an eye on the buildings, as well–'

The Texan and Del Richards, whose saddle-pard, Matheus, had but recently been buried, said nothing. They both knew *someone* had to stay on the place, but the knowledge did nothing to diminish their desperate desire to ride...

Dust whirled along the street and racked horses side-stepped nervously as the cavalcade swept into town and along Main.

It was not such a spectacular entry as some which Hackamore had made. For a start, there were fewer riders. But it was, none the less, just as dramatic. The more so, perhaps, in that each man was grim-faced, tight-lipped, and only talked when absolutely necessary.

They pulled up in a cloud of dust in front of the Yucca. A few men on the board-walks watched them for a moment only, concluding that this bunch was just hitting town for a drinking session or maybe a game.

There were five men behind Frank, Paul and Jed, and now Kearney turned to them as he stepped from leather.

'Look after the horses, boys, and keep

anyone from comin' in, once the shootin's started – even Toomis!'

'You say the word, Frank,' Jim Grady growled, 'an' we'll bring our guns inside!'

Frank's head moved in a decisive, negative gesture. 'The less there are of us, the smaller targets we'll make. You all come in an' they couldn't help kill some of you–'

'It's a lot yo're askin' of us, boss,' Grady replied, 'but we kin take orders as you well know. All I say is, if you three ain't out two minutes after the shootin' starts, *then we come in!*'

Frank nodded and gave them a spare grin. A flicker of admiration showed in Paul's eyes. However blustering and bull-dozing Frank might be, he did not include fear in his make-up. He, as well as anyone, knew that some of them would die tonight, but it was *his* job to face up to killer lead first; *his* job as boss and owner of the outfit which had suffered at the hands of those men inside.

'Mebbe,' Segal grunted, 'they ain't in there–'

'We'll soon find out,' Frank snarled, turning on his heel and striding across the walk to the bat-wing doors, oblivious of whether the other two were close behind or not.

But Segal, as well as Paul, could move fast when it suited him, and as Frank crossed the crowded, smoke- and noise-filled room,

221

the ramrod and Escort were flanking him, one on either side.

For a few seconds, raucous noise retained its high level pitch. A three-piece orchestra contributed to the din of drinkers and gamblers as men whirled with the percentage girls in an intricate reel.

One man at least must have turned and recognized the deathly purpose in the eyes of the newcomers, for the word travelled faster than a prairie fire, and in a moment, only, men fell back as though an invisible scythe had swept a pathway, and all noise stopped, cut off with a suddenness that might have been comical if it had not foreshadowed tragedy.

There were only four men left at the bar now, which a brief moment ago had been packed. The others pushed, scrambled and fell over each other to get out of the line of fire.

Kearney, bellicose, fighting mad, stood with legs widespread, arms hanging loosely at his sides, regarding the men facing him from under craggy brows.

Red Twitchell almost dropped his glass in his hurry to get his hand down at least to belt level. Charlie Widgeon's fat, greasy face took on a sickly pallor. Jack Cotter's beady eyes moved restlessly from Kearney to Escort – the man he feared more than anyone else. Johnny Rideout, the fourth member of the quartette and a two-gun killer, had managed to move away from the others a few paces and now stood in a half-crouch, knees bent, fingers hooked and ready to grab the butts of his guns.

Kearney's voice boomed out, shattering the sweaty silence like the bellow of a bull.

'All right, Twitchell and Cotter! You too, Widgeon! This is the end of the trail! We know all about how you stole Hackamore's trail-herd and killed three of my riders – knifed to death you dirty, murdering scum–'

'What else do you know?' Twitchell sneered, yet his face had paled somewhat and his lips had thinned down to an all but invisible line. A pulse beat in his cheek, betraying the terrific inner tension of the man.

'We know,' Escort gritted, 'that you and your bunch of skunks aren't even content with stealing and killing men. You make war on women! You killed and burned my parents and the ranch, figuring to make it look like a 'Pache raid–'

'You're through, now, Twitchell,' Kearney rasped, 'you and your fat bastard friend, Widgeon–' But even as he spoke a gun roared, spurting flame and hot lead and acrid smoke.

Amazingly, it was Widgeon who had somehow produced a nickel-plated thirty-eight, hiding his covert movements half behind the backs of Twitchell and Cotter. He fired between them, with a few inches to spare on either side the bullet's path, and, as Kearney teetered on his feet, gun only half-drawn, the others whipped into sudden, climactic action; an action which, for all that it had been delayed by the bitter interchange of words, was as inevitable and irrevocable as the eternal dawning of day.

For an almost incalculable measurement in time, Segal's knowledge that Frank had been hit froze his muscles. But almost at once he moved, firing from the hip with lightning speed and taking Widgeon square in the face with his .45 slug.

For a moment or two the crash of guns was incredible in the confines of that crowd-packed, frightened room. Rideout had drawn both sixes and was blazing at the hanging lamps, extinguishing them with machine-like precision and speed. One bullet must have torn clean through the rope, for the huge reflectored lamp came crashing down on to a table amongst the cringing spectators. But for the fact that the flame had blown out the whole room might well have become a raging inferno.

But Twitchell's gun was out now, likewise Cotter's. Yet, even as Red thumbed back the knurled hammer, he felt the shocking impact of the slug as it took him square in the chest, smashing just below his breastbone and piercing the walls of his left lung. He never knew that it was Paul Escort who had killed him as, slowly, his knees buckled and the gun dropped from his feeble grasp. He flung out an arm towards the bar, vainly trying to steady himself and prevent his body from hitting the puncheon floor. But the effort was as puny and as ineffectual as that of a baby. He was dead when he fell full-length, striking his head on the brass footrail.

Cotter fired in panic, fanning his gun in the approved fashion of many a western desperado. But the method had its disadvantages except at extreme close quarters. During the time Cotter emptied his gun, Paul had fired only one shot, but that one shot had been enough, catching Jack Cotter in the throat and causing him to throw up his arms and pivot on one foot like a heavyweight dancing master performing a difficult turn as he fell forward, half across the grotesquely sprawled body of Red Twitchell.

Both Segal and Escort had moved forward ahead of Frank's swaying figure. Rideout seemed suddenly to realize that the task of shooting at all the lamps was too much for one man in the few seconds of time which he had.

He triggered a fusillade of shots, towards the oncoming figures, and Escort felt a dull, burning pain in his left arm where one of the bullets had hit him. Segal fired and Johnny whipped round like a top, dropping his left-hand gun but not falling.

He whirled with the speed of a snake and, unexpectedly, beat it to the rear door, wrenching at the handle with his free but damaged hand.

A bullet splintered the woodwork an inch from his head. Then he had the door open and was through, his booted feet beating out a desperately urgent tattoo.

Vaguely, as in a dream, Paul was aware that someone behind him had fallen. He knew it must be Frank, but for a moment he could not afford to take his eyes away from the scene ahead. He was unsure, as yet, whether any more of Widgeon's or Twitchell's gunsels were present.

He stood there, calmly surveying the crowded room, his smoking gun held un-waveringly, waiting to draw a bead on anyone brash enough to draw chips in the game at this late hour.

Segal's head came round and his gaze dropped to Frank's outstretched form behind. Then, with a wild cry, half-fearful, half-vengeful, Jed rushed to the rear door through which Rideout had, but a moment ago, raced for his very life.

For a second Segal paused in the dimly lit passage-way. Then, ahead and to one side, he spotted the other door. He ran forward, wrenching it open, and boldly, incautiously plunged into the night-enveloped yard. His eyes, unable to see much as a result of rushing from the still partially lit saloon, took a moment to accustom themselves to the darkness. A moment too long! A moment that almost cost Jed Segal his life!

He saw the shape then, all but indistinguishable from the dark wall of the building, and brought his gun up fast. But not fast enough!

Johnny Rideout, with true owlhoot cunning, had known he would have the advantage if followed quickly by one or even two of them. He had laid his sights on that figure of Hackamore's ramrod from the first split-second it had appeared, dimly illumined at the rear door. He had followed the shape with his gun, his eyes narrowed, and more used to the dark than Segal's by a few seconds.

He waited until he had positively identified the man and then, when Segal brought up his gun, Rideout squeezed the trigger. It was too easy!

He laughed as he watched the ramrod sway drunkenly and hit the rubbish-strewn ground with the impact of an explosion.

Still laughing, Rideout ran round the side of the building and down the alley, hauling up a little as he hit the now crowded street.

There were enough folk on the walks and

others quartering towards the sound of shooting at the Yucca saloon to give Rideout all the cover he needed. Not that he would necessarily be suspected of any complicity in this shenanigans, or, even if he were, no one could do anything about it without questions and producing some proof. Only the marshal would have the authority to do this, and thought of the old Indian fighter caused Rideout to make a swift decision. He had been paid for his share in the big steal, and luckily the money was on him right now, or most of it, the rest being safely cached at the bottom of his saddle-bags, and his horse was tied at the end of the rack, *within arm's length!*

There was nothing to hold him in Lariat now that Widgeon and Twitchell were both dead. If they weren't dead, he thought sardonically, they'd be laid up for months – perhaps indefinitely. No! The best thing to do was to get out now, quietly, while the going was good. There would be no more easy pickings in this neck of the woods for a long time to come, if ever. And the sudden thought of that cool bastard, Escort, the Gentle Gunman as men had tagged him, sent a shiver down the spine of even Johnny Rideout. What Cass and the others would do now he didn't care.

So thinking, Johnny quietly untied his horse and climbed into leather coolly and unhurriedly, putting the bay's head to the stage road north-west...

Inside the Yucca saloon the scene had changed somewhat. There was a renewed and vast babble of voices and apparent confusion. But behind the confusion some pattern of order began to appear. Gib Little, the bar-keep, was sweating with housemen and others to set the place to rights.

The Hackamore riders – Jim Grady, Darnell, Steve, Butch and Rowland – unable to hold off any longer, had rushed in with drawn guns, only to find that the curtain was being rung down on one of the most dramatic shoot-outs that Lariat had ever seen.

Their gazes moved from face to face, finally recognizing Escort, where he bent over the still, stiffening body of Frank lying along six hardwood chairs placed together.

Paul looked up quickly. 'You seen Jed recently?' he asked. 'He took out the back way after one of Twitchell's killers–'

Crick said flatly, 'Frank's daid, ain't he, Escort? Wal, if we ketch the fella Jed's after, they's sure goin' to be another funeral!'

'You stay with Frank and Escort, Crick,' Grady said. 'I'll take the boys through to the back.'

He led the way through the milling, noisy crowd, Darnell, Steve and Butch close behind. Men fell back as they moved to the door, knowing that these Hackamore men were going out to look for Segal.

Paul, unable to do anything for the dead Hackamore owner, straightened up and found himself gazing into the seamed face of John Hooley, the new night marshal.

'Seems like you saved the country some expense and trouble,' he said quietly, indicating the figures of Widgeon, Cotter and Twitchell being carried out.

Paul nodded grimly and glanced down at Kearney's waxen face. 'Not without losses ourselves,' he said softly. 'Frank's dead, as you can see, and I'm fearing for Jed Segal, Hackamore's ramrod–' He broke off, suddenly aware that two of the Hackamore crew were returning, carrying their ramrod between them.

There was a question in Paul's eyes, and Grady said, 'Wal, he ain't daid, Escort, but I don't give much fer his chances. We gotta get him to the doc, *pronto.*'

Crick said, 'No trace of the bustard outside?'

Steve shook his head. 'He's gone, whoever he was – the dirty son!'

Paul said, taking off his coat, 'Put this under Jed's head and one of you get the doc here.'

Butch, a short, dour-faced man, placed Paul's rolled-up coat under the unconscious ramrod's head. 'I'll go roust out Doc Scobie,' he grunted. 'Like you said, Escort, mebbe better not to move Jed again till Scobie's seen him.'

He loped out on his errand and then the doors were shoved inwards violently to allow the entry of Marshal Rich Toomis, his face full of questions, even though he was supposed to be off duty...

CHAPTER XV

Arrow in the Back

A lot had happened, a great deal achieved, and still it needed an hour to dawn.

Escort, work-stained and weary, gratefully accepted the laced coffee from Maria which Rona had asked the Mex girl to fix for them.

Rona sat staring before her, eyes focused on, yet not seeing, the shattered window which had now been temporarily covered with paper.

In a chair across the room, Corinne Devereux huddled, a pathetic-looking figure, tear-stains marring her mascara and rouge.

In the small room across the hall lay the body of Frank Kearney. This Rona knew about, had seen. But beyond that she knew little as yet. Escort had only just gotten through with the chores, which had kept him busy half the night.

He placed the empty coffee cup on a table and built himself a smoke at Rona's small go-ahead signal.

He said, drawing smoke deep down into his lungs, 'I guess you don't know much, as yet, beyond the fact that Frank's dead and Jed's badly wounded?'

She shook her head. 'When you sent Steve and Butch up here for the wagon, they wanted to tell me everything, but somehow I – I couldn't face up to it right then. Also, it was urgent to get Frank's body back here – and Jed as well, if we are going to have a chance to save him.'

Paul marvelled at the calm way she was taking all this. Later, he was to understand more fully. But before he could go on, Corinne suddenly rose to her feet.

'This is your private grief,' she told them in a firmer voice than she had used before. 'I'm going back to town. I guess I know already that Twitchell's dead!' She looked at Paul when she said that, and he nodded soberly, scarcely trusting himself to speak then.

She seemed to have known all along, for her expression did not change. Surprisingly, she said, 'I guess it's just as well and it's the best thing that could have happened for Sarah–'

'I broke the news to Sarah before I left

town,' Escort said. 'If you've got the time and – well, if you could find it in your heart–'

Corinne smiled then. It was a gentle, compassionate smile of pure understanding. 'I'll look in on Sarah and – talk to her, Paul,' she promised. 'Is she still at Trail House?'

'No. She's with a friend – Abby Gates–'

'I know the place,' Corinne said, strangely attractive in her masculine garb. She turned at the door, thanking Rona briefly, and stepped outside, closing the door softly behind her.

Partly to give Paul time to recollect his thoughts, Rona moved across to the liquor table and poured two small glasses of whisky. She handed one to Escort and took the other back to the sofa. Those two drinks, earlier on, had kept her going through this awful night...

'Frank wouldn't have it any other way,' Paul said gently. 'I mean he was man enough to want to go in ahead of us all and tackle those thieves and murderers. Jed and I backed him up, and before Frank had finished tackling them Widgeon produced a hide-out gun and shot Frank. Jed's bullet took Widgeon in the face. One of Twitchell's gang was shooting at the lamps, but he couldn't bust them all. Then Cotter and Twitchell were firing. I took Twitchell first and Cotter next and received a nick myself–'

Rona started to her feet. 'You didn't tell

me you were wounded, Paul! Let me see it–'

He smiled wearily and shook his head. 'It wasn't real bad and Doc Scobie fixed it up *pronto*.' He pulled up the sleeve of his jacket, showing the bandaged arm, and she saw the burned and bloodstained shirt-sleeve. If Paul had not been so punch-drunk with fatigue, his brain almost atrophied, he might have wondered why Rona Kearney exhibited more concern over that superficial wound than she had done over the death of her husband.

Paul sipped his drink. 'Jed got the other of Twitchell's gunsels in one arm, but he beat it out the back way. Jed was after him like a demon, but the snake was waiting outside. He must've shot Jed and then lit out.'

Paul paused a hand wearily over his forehead. 'I guess everything seems kinda fogged after that. The Hackamore boys burst in, and then Hooley, the new night marshal, and Toomis himself. There was a deal of talk an' explanations before everything was sorted out.'

'You sided Frank to the hilt,' Rona said softly. 'You and Jed. No man could ask for greater loyalty, greater courage than that.

'You've already done a lot for us here at Hackamore, Paul. Maybe I shouldn't ask you to do anything else–'

'Name it,' Escort said, 'and its done.'

She smiled briefly at that. 'Maybe you

234

shouldn't promise until you know what you're being let in for–'

'If it's staying on here and helping you all I can 'till you get on your feet again, Mrs Kearney, the answer's still "yes"!'

'I want you to rod the spread, at least until Jed is well, and that may be a long time. I want you to think of me as though I were Frank – as though he were still alive – driving you all to the limits to get a new trail herd ready in record time–'

Paul said: 'There are others more fitted than I to be range-boss–'

She shook her head. 'You wouldn't argue with Frank. You might be surprised and wonder, but you wouldn't object. Don't raise obstacles, Paul–'

He stood up and crossed the room to the sofa, stood looking down into her lovely, upturned face. 'I won't raise any – obstacles. If you figure it's best for you and Hackamore this way, I'll start in tomorrow–'

'It's tomorrow now,' she smiled, glancing through the undamaged windows at the paling sky. 'The first thing you've got to do, Paul, is to get some sleep. How are the others?'

He said: 'Jed's comfortable in blankets on his cot. The boys are taking it in turns watching him, although they're almost dead on their feet. I guess you must be pretty well tuckered out, too, Mrs Kearney.'

'We'll both get some sleep, Paul. Later, tomorrow, we'll have Jed moved over here to the house so I can nurse him!'

'You're a brave woman, Ro–, Mrs Kearney. More than just brave!'

She coloured slightly and dropped her gaze. When she looked up again Paul Escort was already closing the door behind him...

Work from sun-up to sun-down; slogging, sweating in the saddle ten hours a day with no more than a half-hour noon break. Too dog-tired at night to play poker or attempt the comparatively short journey to town. Only later on Saturdays and all day Sundays was there any easing up at all.

This was Sunday, and Paul Escort sat on the pole fence of the big corral, contemplating with no little satisfaction the gargantuan task which had been achieved in less than a week.

Seven hundred head had been rounded up and mavericks branded, and this with a depleted crew. But young Welcome had proved himself a good wrangler. This had been a happy thought, giving the youngster a job he loved and releasing Darnell for cow work.

Paul built another smoke and put his gaze across the range to where a rider approached, leading a bunch of horses on a string.

He recognized Toomis, and quickly identified the geldings as his father's – his own now.

Toomis brought the cavvy into the yard, and at the sound Darnell approached from the outbuildings.

At a word from Paul he began hazing them into the smaller alfalfa corral.

Toomis crooked a leg over his saddle horn, accepting Paul's sack and papers with outstretched hand.

'Thanks for bringing them in, Rich.'

The marshal nodded. 'I found 'em all right, like you said I might, but I figgered it too risky to leave 'em down there. A great temptation to anyone in need of a fresh mount. I hazed 'em back to town yesterday and put 'em in the livery overnight.'

Paul nodded. 'I'll settle with Harvey for the feed bill and lodging. Any news from town, Rich?'

The old marshal grinned. 'Plenty,' he said. 'Hooley's lived up to his rep. and caught Jesse Evans. True, we ain't got no jurisdiction proper, outside the town limits, but he mighty soon turned him over to Commart.

'It was Jesse who took a pot shot at Frank that night–'

Escort looked puzzled for a moment. Then his face cleared. 'Oh, the busted window, eh? I did hear something about it, but not from Mrs Kearney.'

'She saved Frank's life, Paul. I found out,

but I guess she wouldn't tell you *that*.'

'No!'

'Another thing. Cotter ain't daid, but he's bad hurt. He won't ever ride the owlhoot trail again, I figger. Even if he gets off with his life, he'll get a long stretch in the pen, soon as he's well enough to stand trial. Chances are though, he'll swing now we got a written statement from Corinne.'

'I guess I'll drop in later and see her as I'm riding into town to pick up Sarah. Ro–, Mrs Kearney's invited Sarah to stay here indefinitely.'

Toomis nodded, pushing back his hat as though this was only to be expected of such a woman.

'She's goin' to make some lucky guy a wonderful wife, Paul,' he said, and let his gaze remain on Escort's reddening face.

Paul said, 'You mean Sarah?'

And Toomis grinned and said: 'Her too, but I was talkin' of Rona Kearney, as well you know! By the way, how's Jed shapin'? Scobie figgers the son's goin' to live!'

'He sure is, I reckon. He's tough as whang leather an' going along like a prairie fire. Jed Segal's a man to ride with, Rich. Well! What am I thinking of, keeping you there in the saddle? Light down, while I see if the cook'll rustle us a cup of coffee!'

Later, when they emerged from the cook-shack, they saw Rona Kearney on the

238

gallery, and Paul veered his steps towards her, trailing the saddled gelding behind him.

He touched his hat and smiled, and Rona returned his greeting and waved a hand to Toomis across the yard.

'Marshal's brought back some Escort geldings from the old place, ma'am,' Paul told her. 'Darnell's hazed 'em in the alfalfa corral. They're for Hackamore's use long as I stay here—'

'You're not figuring on – quitting?' There was sudden alarm in Rona's voice and in her face. It died away when Escort shook his head and explained.

'I'm not riding further than town – to pick up Sary, if that's all right with you?'

'Oh! Of course.' She breathed her relief in a soft, escaping sigh.

'Would you – would you go to the bank for the men's wages if I give you the cheque?'

'Be glad to.' Paul grinned. 'Only it's Sunday today, and only saloons and a few stores are open.'

'Of course. How stupid of me! But then, every day seems the same—'

'I'll go first thing Monday, Mrs Kearney,' Escort promised. 'None of the boys is goin' to worry if his wages are a day or two late. Fact is, we've been too busy to spend anything, anyway. I'd figgered to let them off the leash next week-end and have themselves a night in town. Tomorrow week we'll be ready to drive the new head to Three Forks.'

'Your arrangements have my approval and blessing,' Rona mocked, and with a swift smile turned and walked back into the house...

'They's another thing,' Toomis drawled, ranging his mount alongside Paul's. 'I ain't yet read you the riot act fer takin' the law into your own hands along with Frank and Segal—'

'All right. Go ahead and get it over with.' Paul smiled.

'Well,' the marshal replied, tugging at his moustaches, 'like John Hooley said, it seems like you done saved the county a deal of time an' money. Corinne Devereux got to Widgeon's safe before I or Hooley ever thought about it. Wouldn't you have said, Paul, that Widgeon, the kingpin in this big steal which apparently was only a taste of things to come, would've had a sizeable pile of *dinero* cached in his safe?'

'I should've thought so,' Paul said cautiously.

Toomis chuckled. 'Thet Corinne's sure smart. Allus did admire her, even though I'm figuring she's broke the law—'

'What do you mean?'

'Why, she calmly gives me a book with lists an' figures an' amounts, provin' Widgeon was behind all this. They even got the thousand head of Hackamore entered up with

240

the amounts alongside – purchased by un-named buyers. *But Corinne says that's all there was in Widgeon's safe,* beyond a few bills of sale and personal papers!'

Escort grinned. It was his turn now. 'Looks like Corinne Devereux is goin' to make some man a real smart wife. That is, if he's not *too* old and *too* concerned with what other folks might say–'

'Bigawd!' Toomis said slowly, as his leath-ern cheeks took on a rosy glow. 'Bigawd, Escort,' he repeated, and then: 'But she'd never have an old fool like me! Besides which–'

'Of course,' Paul said pleasantly, 'if you figure just because she's worked in a saloon, mebbe made a few mistakes – well, dammit, man! Suppose she *was* Twitchell's girl? She hadta have *some* protection in a frontier town like Lariat! I guess none of us is so good we can go around pointing the finger at others!' he ended soberly.

Toomis rode in silence, gazing ahead, not seeing the country, but perhaps glimpsing something of the life ahead which could – *might* be his, had he the courage to act!

He thought he would sooner face up single-handed to a score of war-painted braves than attempt what Paul had suggested.

But by the time they reached Lariat, Marshal Rich Toomis knew that, once again, he was going to call on all his reserves of courage!...

On Monday morning Escort took one of the wagons and made his second journey to town within twenty-four hours.

Not only was he going to tote back wages for the crew, but stores as well, hence his choice of the spring-wagon.

He tooled the wagon and team along at an easy pace, thinking about Rona, about Corinne and Toomis, wondering if the latter would do as Paul had suggested. On the face of it, perhaps, it might seem they would make an incongruous couple, with different outlooks and values and incompatible standards. But Escort had seen more deeply into both of them than most people and had found with little surprise that both were warm-hearted and fair-minded underneath the tough protecting exteriors which they had been forced to assume.

That, in itself, did not necessarily make for wedded bliss, Paul figured soberly, but it sure went a hell of a long way!

When he brought the rig on to Main he was mildly surprised to notice a big crowd outside the stage office. He could see the top of the stage itself and the empty driver's box, and, between the milling crowd, caught glimpses of the drooping, saline-flecked team.

This stage had hit town in a hurry, and there was more than the usual crowd of sightseers and loafers pressing round today.

As Paul reined in on the outskirts of the crowd he caught sight of Toomis and wondered what could be amiss.

He climbed down from the wagon, after hitching the ribbons round the whip-stock, and several men, turning their heads, gave greeting and allowed him passage through the crowd.

Toomis lifted his gaze from the ground and greeted Escort. The stage-driver, his shotgun guard and Toomis were standing in a tight arc around the body of a man stretched out on the board-walk. Paul could see the man was dead, firstly because of his utter stillness and stiff rigidity; secondly, because an arrow still jutted out from under his left shoulder blade. It must have pierced his lungs, probably his heart as well, Paul thought.

Toomis turned the corpse half on its side, giving Paul his first clear look at the man's face. He stared for a moment, and then sudden recognition came, even though the dead man's face was waxen and his eyes closed.

'That's the other hombre who was siding Twitchell, Cotter and Widgeon,' Paul said, speaking to the three principle men in front of him. 'The one who escaped through the back and laid for Jed Segal!'

Toomis nodded. 'We already figgered that,

Paul. Seems like his name was John Rideout, accordin' to a letter we found in his pockets–'

'Does this mean 'Paches are breaking out?' Escort interrupted, but the marshal shook his grizzled head.

'Bat here,' he said, indicating the stagedriver, 'figgered he saw a half-dozen bucks four-five miles down the road. When he brought the stage up there was no Injuns, but this hombre was lying stretched out, daid, with thet arrer in his back. He sure had a heap of gold in his pockets–'

'The Injuns didn't rob him then–?'

Toomis grinned sardonically. 'What's the use of gold to them? But they stole his horse and guns. Something which all that money couldn't buy for 'em – specially the guns and shells.'

Paul nodded slowly and traversed his gaze to the driver's face. 'This didn't look like a wholesale uprising then, to you?'

Bat grinned, showing yellow teeth. He shook his head. 'I seen plen'y Injuns painted fer war, same as the marshal here. This wasn't no more than a small bunch o' hunters, riding a wide sweep from their camp in the Smoke Signals.

'As I figger it, they spotted a lone rider an' couldn't resist knockin' him off to steal horse an' guns; but they wasn't painted fer war, an' he's still got his hair, like you kin see!'

'He figgered he was being plenty smart, I guess,' Toomis drawled. 'Mebbe he was at that, if it hadn't been fer them 'Paches. I guess Johnny Rideout's been well and truly paid now for tryin' to drygulch Jed Segal...'

CHAPTER XVI

Confession and Declaration

For the last two-three days the Hackamore crew had made prodigious efforts to complete the round-up of prime, three-four-year-old stuff.

There were still plenty of cattle roaming Hackamore land, of course, but it had meant riding further afield, with a depleted crew, and chousing well-fed steers loath to leave good graze and water for the holding grounds.

During that hectic time, when a ranny was in the saddle more hours than not – even including sleeping – Paul saw little of Rona, the now-established owner of Hackamore under Frank's will.

Kearney lay buried on his own ground, beyond the windbreak of cottonwoods and alongside the other Hacakmore men who had fallen in defending Kearney's stock and property. Once, Paul and Crick Rowland had visited the mounds, toting the grave-markers which had been rudely fashioned and which bore the names and approximate dates of birth.

Paul had been surprised to see that flowers – wild azaleas and oleanders – had been strewn over the graves. At once he saw Rona's hand in this. She had made no discrimination, not favouring Frank's grave, but had distributed the floral tributes impartially.

Tonight he sat perched atop the corral smoking a *cigarrito* and thinking that he would have to get a few more hands to fill the gap. And if suitable men could not be found in Lariat, then no doubt they could pick up a few foot-loose, experienced hands in Three Forks when they got there with the herd.

One thing, Segal was coming along fine, although it would still be a long while before he would fork a horse or ride for any length of time.

Soon, now, Jed would be fit enough to move back to the bunkhouse, once the dressings and the nursing became no longer necessary. He thought maybe he would go up to the house tonight, now, and have a talk with Jed.

Paul spun the glowing stub across the yard and climbed down from his perch. Everything here was so peaceful now, it seemed impossible to recollect the full extent of those dramatic events a few weeks back.

In the bunkhouse some of the boys were setting in on a game, the rest were with the herd. Paul moved across to the lighted house, suddenly aware of the fact that he was using Segal as an excuse! True enough, there *were* things that he wanted to discuss: this hiring of new hands; for the summer months were always busy ones on a big spread and there would be the fall shipment to think about.

But, in his heart of hearts, Escort knew it was Rona he really wanted to see. It had been as though she were deliberately keeping out of his way of late. What news he had had of her had been mostly through Sarah, whose home was now firmly established here at Hackamore.

Perhaps Rona was still nursing her silent grief, Paul thought. After all, she had not been long a widow. But yet...

He ascended the steps, crossing the gallery, whose floor was reticulated with lamplight shining through the screen door.

As he passed through into the hall the living room door opened and Rona stood there, the strong contrast of light and shadow accentuating her full-bodied beauty.

She said: 'Come in for a drink, Paul. We haven't seen much of you lately. I know how busy you must have been—'

He removed his hat, following her into the big living room which now, with a few recent feminine touches, seemed cosier and not quite so vast.

He took the drink she offered, grateful for it, for in ten days he had not visited Lariat – not to tarry.

'How's Jed today – Rona?' He couldn't hold back from calling her by her own name any longer. At least, not when they were alone. In front of the men it was still, 'Mrs Kearney, ma'am.'

She looked particularly wonderful tonight, he thought. She wore a gown of bronze-blue taffeta shot with gold, tight-fitting at the low corsage and flaring out to the ground, fire seeming to strike it with every movement of her body. Bronze-blue pendants dangled from the lobes of her small ears, and a water-silk ribbon and cameo tightly encircled the column of her throat.

She smiled. 'He's doing fine, Paul. Much longer and he won't be needing a nurse. I guess he's raring to go!'

Paul nodded. 'I guess he is, but he's not doing any riding work for a long time yet.'

She moved a vase of flowers a couple of inches without real purpose, without even being aware of what she did.

'You seem to have made a good job of taking over the reins,' she said, and when Paul flushed she added: 'That wasn't teasing, it was meant as a compliment–'

She stood close to him now. Somehow the physical as well as the spiritual distance had closed between them suddenly. He could see her breasts rising and falling rapidly under the sheath of taffeta. Her eyes, misted, were on his face, her lips invitingly parted. And in a second she was in his arms, straining towards him as his mouth sought hers.

Passionate yet gentle; earthly yet spiritual; the merging of two flames into one. Yet it was Rona who gently pulled away first, her eyes at once starry but filled with pain.

'You don't know the kind of woman I am, Paul,' she said, her voice low and husky with emotion. He would have taken her again, but she raised her hand gently, holding him off and shaking her head fiercely.

'No! Paul! Listen to me! It won't work. You don't know me, I tell you. I married Frank – not because I loved him – I hated him – I married him to destroy him like – like a *tarantula*–'

'This is crazy talk, Rona!' Paul said harshly.

'No, Paul. Hear me out! Perhaps there was *some* excuse for what I did. I don't know. All I know is that I have done wrong, and now Frank – whatever his faults – is dead in a cold, earthen grave!'

He caught her hands then, fiercely, drawing her towards him.

'I won't listen to this crazy talk, Rona. I know–'

'You don't know that I married Frank just to break him–'

'*Why?*'

'He – he – it was a long time ago, Paul.' She was crying quietly now, and Escort felt the pain in his breast as he watched her and listened.

'I had a brother – Steve. He was my twin. Do you know what that means, Paul? Can you possibly understand how *close* we were – almost the same flesh? Our faces were alike, our minds almost the same – it was as though we only had one heart between us.'

She broke off, and Paul picked up a whisky glass and offered it to her. When she shook her head he growled, 'Drink it, Rona!'

She swallowed the liquor and shuddered slightly, but it enabled her to get a grip on herself. When she continued it was in a calmer, steadier voice.

'Steve got in with William Bonney, Paul. Billy the Kid. He only rode with him a couple of times, I think. That was back in Texas. The next time he rode he stole a horse, and Frank killed him – shot him in the back while he was riding away!

'I was only sixteen then, Paul. But I loved Steve more than anything else in the world.

Oh, he was a wild boy, but Frank never gave him a chance. From that moment something died right here inside me, a part of me, I guess, and I swore I'd get even with Frank Kearney even though it might take me years to do it.

'I kept an eye on Hackamore and later followed them up here when Frank came to look for bigger grazing lands. It took me nearly two years from the time I first began to cultivate his acquaintance to the time we were married. Somehow or other, Paul, I was determined to *ruin* Frank, cost what it might!'

'Have you forgotten that you saved his life that night when Evans, if it were him, tried to shoot Frank? Do you think, Rona, that such an act counts for nothing?

'Whatever you had in mind, even if it *was* to ruin Frank, no one would blame you for that. Why, my dear, a man would have strapped a gun on himself and ridden out and *killed* under those circumstances. It's been done a thousand times before and will be done again. Now, what other foolish notions have you in your beautiful head?'

She stared at him, wide-eyed, her fingers digging into his arms through the jacket.

'But isn't that enough, Paul? Isn't it enough that I married Frank, not only under false pretences, but with evil in my heart? Now, see, because of that I am owner of the vast

Hackamore spread–'

'And *that* has been the one reason why I have been scared to speak to you until tonight, Rona,' Paul murmured in her ear.

'Any wrong that was in your heart or mind has been fully expiated when you saved Frank's life. Toomis told me about that, so I know it's true. You could have stood back and done nothing, and for you the problem would have been solved and your hands would have been clean.

'Instead, you elected to shout a warning. You even fired the gun you were holding and caused Evans to abandon the attempt, at least, temporarily.

'No, Rona. You must see this thing in its true light. You are a much better woman than you think. There is no evil in your heart. But I thank God that you have told me because–'

'Because why, Paul?' she asked softly with shining eyes.

'Because,' he answered her, 'it is almost the one thing which could have given me the courage to ask – to ask–'

'My darling,' she whispered. 'The answer is "yes" with all my heart and soul...'

This Large Print Book, for people
who cannot read normal print,
is published under the auspices of

THE ULVERSCROFT FOUNDATION